All C... Figure... How A Woman Was Supposed To Act Around The Stranger She Planned To Marry.

She *had* to make the man fall in love with her. That was the crux of the matter. But she didn't think she could manage a coy look if her life depended on it.

But her life *did* depend on it. Her life and the lives of her two babies.

She was going to have to make herself irresistible. She would clean like crazy, cook something unforgettable, show off her great kids and he wouldn't be able to resist.

And she would have him in wedding clothes by the end of the week....

Dear Reader,

LET'S CELEBRATE FIFTEEN YEARS
OF SILHOUETTE DESIRE...

with some of your favorite authors and new stars of tomorrow.
For the next three months, we present a spectacular lineup
of unforgettably romantic love stories—led by three
MAN OF THE MONTH titles.

In October, Diana Palmer returns to Desire with
The Patient Nurse, which features an unforgettable hero.
Next month, Ann Major continues her bestselling CHILDREN
OF DESTINY series with *Nobody's Child.* And in December,
Dixie Browning brings us her special brand of romantic
charm in *Look What the Stork Brought.*

But Desire is not only MAN OF THE MONTH! It's new
love stories from talented authors Christine Rimmer,
Helen R. Myers, Raye Morgan, Metsy Hingle and new star
Katherine Garbera in October.

In November, don't miss sensuous surprises from BJ James,
Lass Small, Susan Crosby, Eileen Wilks and Shawna Delacorte.

And December will be filled with Christmas cheer from
Maureen Child, Kathryn Jensen, Christine Pacheco,
Anne Eames and Barbara McMahon.

Remember, here at Desire we've been committed to bringing
you the very best in unforgettable romance and sizzling
sensuality. And to add to the excitement of fifteen wonderful
years, we offer the chance for you to win some wonderful
prizes. Look in the pages at the end of the book for details.

And may we have many more years of happy reading together!

Melissa Senate

Senior Editor

Please address questions and book requests to:
Silhouette Reader Service
U.S.: 3010 Walden Ave., P.O. Box 1325, Buffalo, NY 14269
Canadian: P.O. Box 609, Fort Erie, Ont. L2A 5X3

RAYE MORGAN
WIFE BY CONTRACT

SILHOUETTE *Desire*
Published by Silhouette Books
America's Publisher of Contemporary Romance

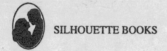 SILHOUETTE BOOKS

ISBN 0-373-76100-7

WIFE BY CONTRACT

Printed in U.S.A.

Books by Raye Morgan

Silhouette Desire

Embers of the Sun #52
Summer Wind #101
Crystal Blue Horizon #141
A Lucky Streak #393
Husband for Hire #434
Too Many Babies #543
Ladies' Man #562
In a Marrying Mood #623
Baby Aboard #673
Almost a Bride #717
The Bachelor #768
Caution: Charm at Work #807
Yesterday's Outlaw #836
The Daddy Due Date #843
Babies on the Doorstep #886
Sorry, the Bride Has Escaped #892
*Baby Dreams #997
*A Gift for Baby #1010
*Babies by the Busload #1022
*Instant Dad #1040
Wife by Contract #1100

*The Baby Shower

Silhouette Romance

Roses Never Fade #427

RAYE MORGAN

favors settings in the West, which is where she has spent most of her life. She admits to a penchant for Western heroes, believing that whether he's a rugged outdoorsman or a smooth city sophisticate, he tends to have a streak of wildness that the romantic heroine can't resist taming. She's been married to one of those Western men for twenty years and is busy raising four more in her Southern California home.

One

Joe Camden hadn't expected to get a lump in his throat. Sentimental emotions weren't usually his style. But something happened when he got out of his car and looked down at the old ramshackle house.

Home. That was what it was, even though he'd been gone for fifteen years, even though he'd run as fast and as far away as he could when he'd had the chance.

"Ah, you'll miss it," Annie Andrews had said, shaking her gray head and laughing at him the day he took off. He'd stopped by to get supplies for his hitch-hiking odyssey in her tiny combination post office and general store. "Alaska will call you back."

"Not me," he'd said, sure enough of that to grin at her. "It's bright lights and big cities for me from now on."

"And girls," she added for him, laughing again.

"It's true, we don't have enough girls here for you young men. It's no wonder you all run off."

His wide mouth twisted in a half smile as he remembered that day and thought of all the things that he'd been through since. Now he was back, and Annie was half-right. The Alaska grandeur, the white peaks, the forest green meadows, the water tumbling through the gorges still had the power to stir him. But it really wasn't home any longer. He belonged in L.A.

Still, everything was the same as ever. It hardly looked as though anything had changed since he'd left. The old house where his brother, Greg, still lived looked as beat-up as ever. Evidence suggested Greg was as allergic to responsibility as their father had been—but then, Joe hadn't expected anything else. In fact, that was why he'd come back.

A rustling caught his ear, and he glanced toward the nearby trees. He caught a glimpse of what looked like brown fur in the underbrush, and the past came tumbling back to him even more strongly.

"Champ," he murmured, remembering his childhood pet, the energetic brown dog who would hide in the bushes and then jump out at him, licking his face and wriggling in his arms. Without thinking, without wanting to remember that Champ had died when he was eighteen, he went toward the brush and stuck his hand into the leaves where he'd seen the movement, as though he could find that puppy just as he had so often so many years ago, as though he thought he might be able to reach back into yesterday and pull the dog up by the scruff of the neck.

"Champ?"

Champ didn't answer, but something with teeth bit

down on his hand, and he yanked it back, swearing. "Ouch. What the hell...?"

A small boy emerged from the underbrush, running as fast as his chubby little legs could take him, his brown hair bouncing on his head as he ran straight for the house.

"Hey," Joe called after him, but the little boy didn't turn. He ran on, stumbling but not giving up, as though the devil himself were after him, aiming to snatch him up and carry him off. Joe realized, with a twinge of regret, that to this kid, he probably was the devil.

"Hey, I won't hurt you," he called after him half-heartedly, frowning as he looked down at the unmistakable imprint of teeth on his hand. He'd seen them often enough before, when he and his brother, Greg, were young and he would pin Greg down and Greg would fight back any way he could.

He shook his head as though to clear it. Too many things were echoing the past, and he was beginning to feel a little weird about it. There was no Champ, and this kid wasn't Greg. But what was he doing at Greg's house?

He started down the hill after him. Before he'd gone more than a few feet, a woman appeared, coming out through the front door to stand on the porch. The sight of her surprised Joe, pulling him up short.

She raised her hand to shade her eyes against the slice of noonday sun that hit her face. "Rusty?" she called out to the boy as he raced toward her. Then she looked up and saw Joe, and she seemed to freeze, just as he had done.

He stared. He'd never seen anything like her in Alaska before. Out here, conditions were rough and the women dressed appropriately. This woman wore a white wool suit with heels and stockings. Her silvery blond hair shimmered around her face in a chic, professional style, catching the sunbeams, setting off a glow, so that she seemed to be standing in a shaft of golden light.

He shook his head slowly, drawn even more out of sync with this situation. It just didn't fit his experience of Alaska, didn't fit with his past, didn't fit with what he knew of his brother's present. He felt unbalanced. Who in the world was this woman, and what was she doing in his brother's house?

Chynna Sinclair saw the man coming down from the rise, saw the car in the background, and her mouth went dry.

"Oh, darn it," she whispered softly to herself. He'd already seen Rusty. There was going to be no way to hide the boy now, even for the first few minutes while they got acquainted.

Rusty reached her and threw himself against her, wrapping his little arms around her knees and burying his face against her skirt. She looked down at him and tousled his hair lovingly.

Oh, well. Maybe it was best that they get the worst over with right from the beginning. She looked out at the man again. Why was he just standing there, staring at her?

"Come on into the house," she told her son, gently untangling his arms from her legs. "Come stay with Kim while I talk to the man."

Maybe if she got the kids quieted down and playing with something, she would have time to talk to him and prepare him....

But whom was she kidding? There was no more

time to hide, to make up stories. She'd been putting if off all during the plane ride from Chicago, all during the flight from Anchorage in the little six-seater plane; even in the ride from the landing strip, when the pilot had kindly borrowed a car to get them here, she'd told herself it was time to make a decision on what she was going to say when she saw him. But now it was too late. He'd already seen Rusty. He already knew that the mail-order bride he'd ordered, the pretty young woman he expected, had brought along some baggage she hadn't warned him about.

Hurrying her son inside, she settled him and his little sister with coloring books in the living room and went back out on the porch. He was still standing there, staring at the house. She hesitated, thinking she should walk out to greet this large male she hoped would be her husband soon, but knowing her heels would sink in the mud if she tried it. She knew she wasn't dressed for the area, but she'd done it on purpose. This was a selling job she was going to have to do here, and image, as her boss used to tell her in Chicago, was everything. She waited instead, fingers curling around the post at the top of the stairs, her heart beating like a wild thing in her chest.

What if he didn't want her? What if he didn't want her kids? She had to convince him. There was no choice in the matter.

She still didn't know what she was going to say. This was so hard to explain on the spur of the moment. It was the sort of thing it would be better for him to learn about gradually, as he got to know her, as he got to know the kids. As he got to know them, he would understand. But how could he possibly understand when it was dropped in his lap in one large lump like this?

Taking a deep breath, she forced a smile. "Hi, there," she called to him. "I guess you missed us at the landing strip. The pilot drove us over."

As though she'd flicked a switch and brought him back to life, he started walking slowly toward her.

She wet her lips and smiled a welcome. "I hope you don't mind. Your house wasn't locked and I...I went on in."

He was closer now and she could see his face, and something inside her relaxed. She hadn't allowed herself to believe in the picture he'd sent her. It showed a man so handsome, she'd told herself to assume it was taken ten years ago, or was a phony in some other way.

But no. The picture hadn't lied. This was the same man, all right. In fact, with his broad shoulders and dark hair and glittering blue eyes, he looked even better than he had in the photograph. He wore crisp jeans and a leather bomber jacket, and neither was old or dirty. They looked, in fact, startlingly fashionable for this neighborhood.

She'd had a picture in her mind of what she would find here, and this wasn't really it. She'd imagined a farmer-hunter type, rough-hewn and bashful. This man was none of those things. This man looked a little too good to be real.

He'd reached the porch and was coming up the stairs, his face drawn into a frown as he looked her over, as though she puzzled him, or annoyed him, or something. She stepped forward quickly.

"Hi," she said, holding out her hand and bringing

back her quick smile. "I'm Chynna Sinclair, and I'm very glad to be here."

He took her hand and seemed to marvel at it. Then he looked into her face and shook his head. "What's going on here?" he asked her, searching her eyes for answers. "Where's Greg?"

But his last question was drowned out by a shriek from inside the house and then by the sound of something breaking. Chynna whirled, glanced at him quickly and muttered, "Uh...I'd better see what happened" before running in to tend to her children.

Joe followed her, then stopped just inside the entryway, turning slowly to take it all in. The house was just the same as it had been before he'd left. Greg hadn't changed a thing.

He could hear Chynna settling some sort of argument that was going on in the next room, but he didn't pay any attention. He was looking at the picture of his grandfather that still hung on the wall, his flinty pioneer eyes still staring at his grandson with the same old sense of disapproval; at the snow shovel propped in the corner, the one that always gave him splinters that lasted longer in his skin than the snow lasted on the ground; at the tall, elegant breakfront where his mother had kept her precious dishes and porcelain figurines. Only a few were left, the ones she didn't care about. He supposed she'd taken all the rest when she moved to Anchorage, five years before. Nothing had changed.

Nothing—except Joe himself.

The woman who called herself Chynna Sinclair came back into the entryway, and he looked up, blinking, wondering how she managed to seem to carry the sunlight with her. She was certainly a pretty thing, but she looked so out of place here in the Alaskan wilderness. He supposed she must be Greg's girlfriend, though he could hardly imagine where Greg could have met her. Greg wouldn't go near the city, and this was city bred, all the way. But then, what did he really know about his brother these days? If only Greg were here, these things could be cleared up right away.

"I...I have to introduce you to my children," she said, stuttering slightly, and he looked into her eyes with surprise. Why was she so nervous? "This is Rusty. He's five. And Kim is three."

He looked down at the two sets of eyes, both open very wide, looking as though awe had struck them silly, and he smiled and nodded. "Hi, kids," he said casually, his mind still on the woman.

"Children," she told them, "this is Mr. Greg Camden. I...I think you should call him Mr. Camden for now."

Joe's gaze shot up to meet hers. She thought he was Greg? This was crazy. "No, wait a minute...."

She grabbed hold of his arm, stopping him from speaking, and said to her children, "You go on back and color for a few minutes. I have to talk to Mr. Camden."

She was trembling. He could feel it but he had no idea why she would be so emotional about this. Still, her fingers dug into his arm as the children filed out, and he waited, since that was what she seemed to want.

He gazed down into her soft hair, catching a hint of the scent of roses. She seemed small, slender, and for a moment he was reminded of the time he'd found a young silver fox caught in a rusty trap in the pine forest. It had trembled, too, as he'd used one hand to quiet it while working it free with the other. That had been a fool thing to do. He'd known the whole time that the fox could turn at any moment and lash out at him, hurt him badly. But it had been something he'd had to do. The fox had struggled at first, but then it had lain still, and once free, it had streaked off into the woods. Joe had never seen it again.

Her children had finally straggled out of the room, and her head turned. Her dark eyes met his, but there was nothing wary in them, nothing fearful. They were huge and soft and warm, but there was a challenging look to them that caught him by surprise and made him wonder if he'd only imagined that she was nervous. Maybe she'd been shivering from the cool air.

"Okay," she said crisply. "We can talk."

"Listen," he began, anxious to get this identity thing cleared up.

But she shook her head, still clinging to his arm, looking up into his face and talking very fast. "No, you listen. I know this isn't fair. I know I should have told you. But...but this is the way it is and the way it has to be. If you don't want us, I'll understand. But you have to give us a chance. You can't just turn us away without giving us a chance."

He stared at her, completely at sea. He had no idea what she was talking about.

"I didn't tell you about Rusty and Kim," she went on earnestly, "and that was wrong. But I wanted you to see them before you made up your mind. I wanted you to get to know them. They're good kids—they really are. They'll grow on you—you'll see."

A shriek from the other room made her wince, but she forced a smile, despite the fact that Joe was shaking his head.

"Listen, kids are not my thing—" he began.

"I know," she broke in, throwing out one arm as though that were the most natural reaction in the world. "Of course not. Living out here in Alaska, you probably hardly see kids. So you don't really know, do you?"

He made a face and shrugged. This conversation was crazy, but she looked so cute trying to convince him, he wasn't sure he wanted it to end. "I was a kid once," he reminded her.

Her eyes brightened. "Kids have improved since then," she told him artfully. "You'll see."

He grinned, appreciating her spirit though he knew better than to believe her. "You know what?" he said. "There's no use trying to convince me. Because I'm not Greg."

Her eyes widened, and she stared at him for a long, long moment. Then a look of skepticism crept over her face.

"Oh, I see," she said, her eyes turning as chilly as her tone. "You're going to try to get out of this that way, are you?"

"No," he said, half laughing. He ran a hand through his dark hair and gazed down at her, perplexed. "Look, it's true. I'm not Greg. And I'm not even sure why you're here."

"I'm here to marry you. Remember?"

"Marry...?" Words failed him, and he lost his breath. All he could do was stand there, staring down at her. The word had hit him like a flash of lightning, shutting off all thought processes as the shock skittered through his body.

"Yes, marry." She tried to smile, but his reaction had thrown her off her game. "That was the plan."

He shook his head, struggling to put his feelings into words. "Oh, no, I can't believe that. Marriage..." He thought of his brother and his isolated ways and shook his head again. "No, that can't be."

Her eyes narrowed, and her pretty mouth set. Turning, she whipped an envelope out of her purse and handed it to him. "Then what is this?" she demanded.

The envelope was slit open at the top. A letter was tucked inside, along with a photograph. The letter was from his brother. The photograph was of Joe.

"A deal is a deal, mister," she told him firmly as he unfolded the letter and glanced at it. "You contracted for a bride. You looked through an extensive catalog and you chose me. And here I am."

Words still stuck in his throat. He looked at her. He looked at the picture. He looked back at her. And nothing came out of his mouth. If he took her at her word, if he took what she was saying literally—well, then she had to be a mail-order bride. He swore softly, shaking his head. What had he done, stepped back in time? People didn't do things like this anymore. Did they?

Grasping at straws, he waved the envelope at her. "This is a joke, right?"

She stared at him for a moment, then tossed her head and turned into the kitchen, taking off her suit jacket as she went. "Is there an apron in here somewhere?" she asked, then grabbed a large tea towel and tied it around her waist without waiting for an answer.

"What are you doing?" he asked, following her, still clutching the envelope, still feeling very much at sea.

She looked up at him with cool defiance. "I'm going to make you something to eat. I'm going to cook."

He frowned. "You don't need to cook for me."

"Why not? Aren't you hungry?"

He hesitated. It had been a long time since he'd eaten breakfast. "Well, yes, but..."

"Then I will cook for you," she said, opening the refrigerator and staring inside. "Consider it a form of audition for the job."

He couldn't hold back a grin. "This is crazy," he said, shaking his head.

She nodded, pulling eggs and bacon out and placing them on the counter. "I think so, too," she said coolly. "But you seem to need to be convinced."

He slumped back against the counter, watching her, pushing back the erotic fantasies that threatened to break into his thoughts. He had an urge to pinch himself. Could he be dreaming? Talk about dreams come true—here was this woman, offering herself up to...

No, he wouldn't think about it. That would only end up getting him into big trouble—trouble he didn't need.

"I don't mean to ridicule you, you know," he told her softly. "But I just can't believe that a woman like you has to resort to something like...like mail order...to get a man." He grimaced. "It just doesn't compute."

She spun and confronted him. "Look. You picked me out of the catalog. You must have liked something about me. You wrote me that nice letter and sent me your picture. You signed a contract with the agency." She searched his blue eyes, looking for answers. "You sent money for my plane fare. What did you think? That this was all a game? That I would never actually show up?"

He started shaking his head before she was finished

and kept shaking it. "That was my brother Greg who did all that," he tried to explain once again. "My name is Joe. It wasn't me."

She grabbed his hand and looked up into his face, her eyes huge with determined entreaty. "Give me a chance," she said softly. "Please. I'll be a good wife. And my kids..." She shook her head, and for a moment he was afraid her eyes would fill with tears. "They're good kids. You just wait. They won't be any trouble at all. You're going to love them."

Loving kids had never been one of his goals, but he had to admit he was beginning to feel a definite temptation in other directions. He liked her big brown eyes and the way her breasts filled out the pale pink silk shell she wore and the way her lower lip seemed to pout when she was annoyed with him. His mind began to wander for just a moment, mulling over what it would be like to order up a woman like this from a catalog and have her appear on the doorstep, ready to be a wife. It was a caveman dream, but he kind of liked it.

But before he had time to indulge in it for more than a few seconds, a cry came from the living room, and suddenly a huge crash shook the house.

"Yeah, those adorable kids," he muttered to himself as she jerked away, spun and started for the living room. "I just can't get enough of how cute they are."

But he started after her. Until Greg showed up, he guessed it was his job to act as a sort of surrogate husband here. Though before he made any commitments, maybe he ought to think over just exactly what that was going to entail.

His gaze fell on the letter she'd left lying on the table, and he stopped, hesitating. It wasn't nice to read other people's mail. But what the hell. He had a situation here. Reaching out, he took hold of the letter by the corner, as though he wasn't sure it wasn't contagious, and carried it over to where the light from the window was the brightest. Gingerly, he unfolded it and began to read.

It was the letter Greg had written to Chynna, but it didn't sound like his brother at all. The handwriting was Greg's. So was the signature at the bottom of the page. But the thoughts he'd written down sounded like someone else's entirely. There were references to loneliness and love of the land, and those he could readily identify with his brother. But there was also talk of soul mates and walking hand in hand through life together, which made Joe want to laugh out loud.

What did he do, copy these romantic phrases from a book? he wondered to himself as he looked them over. The closest thing to a soul mate he could think of for Gregg might be a rabid wolverine.

He frowned, shaking his head. He and Greg had never been close. In some ways, they were the typical Cain and Abel siblings. Whenever Joe said black, Greg claimed white. When Joe wanted peace, Greg turned his radio on high screech. When Greg came home late, like as not, Joe would have locked the door. When Greg spoke, Joe tended to answer him sarcastically, and when Joe laughed, Greg found a way to turn the mood surly.

Now that Joe had been away all these years, he sometimes regretted the way they couldn't get along. He'd even decided, a few years back, that the rift between them was childish and should be over now that they were men, so he'd come home. But nothing had changed. If anything, Greg had grown moodier and more aloof. The planned-for reconciliation hadn't panned out.

And now this recluse, this mountain man was figuring to take himself a wife, was he? The situation made no sense at all. And yet it was obvious Chynna was right when she claimed to be here because Greg had...good Lord! Ordered her from a catalog?

His brother, Greg, was preparing to take himself this lovely woman as a wife.

"Over my dead body," Joe muttered aloud, thinking of Chynna and her wide, hopeful gaze. "It can't happen. I'd better get her out of here as soon as possible."

Unfortunately, that was going to be more difficult than it might seem. Unless there had been a radical and unexpected change, the only way out by air would be on the mail plane, and who knew what the schedule was these days. There was probably no other way out except by truck or car, and he couldn't leave. He had to find Greg.

He might as well resign himself to the fact that she was going to be staying overnight at least.

But then she would have to go. It would be much too dangerous to let her stay.

Two

This wasn't working out the way she'd planned it.

Chynna picked up the small table and vase, which luckily was made of some sort of sturdy ceramic that didn't break easily. After a nervous glance at the goldfish bowl on the hutch at the window, which luckily hadn't been touched, she scolded her children for their behavior, her nervousness making her words a little sharper than they might usually have been. Kim looked up at her warily and popped a thumb in her mouth. Rusty's lower lip began to quiver. Chynna noted that fact, hesitated, then sighed regretfully and drew him to her.

Her kids were usually so good. She'd been so sure they would charm this man she'd come to marry, make him happy to have them as a family. Instead, things were slipping out of control.

"What is it, Rusty?" she asked, her instincts telling

her that something other than the overturned table was
bothering him. As she looked down into his earnest
face, it seemed to crumple beneath her gaze, and he
threw himself against her.

"I bit the man," Rusty told her, sobbing quietly into
her shoulder. "I bit him."

She frowned, holding him close and trying to understand what it was he was saying. "What man? Greg
Camden?" He nodded, his face pressed into the hol-
low. "You bit him? You mean with teeth?"

Rusty drew back so that she could see him, made a
face, then clamped his teeth together with a snap.
"Like that," he said, nodding tearfully. "I'm sorry,
Mommy. I d-d-didn't mean to."

Chynna recalled the sight of her son racing down
the hill and Greg coming behind him and she winced.
"Did he do anything to you?" she asked anxiously,
studying his dirt-streaked face.

"I was hiding," he said, gulping back a sob. Huge
drops of water stood in his eyes. "I thought he was
going to grab me. So I did this." He snapped his jaws
together again, his eyes brightening. Obviously, he
was beginning to enjoy the reenactments. "I did it
hard," he said with just a hint of satisfaction. "He
yelled."

"Oh, Rusty," she cried in horror, pulling him to
her chest and rocking him. "I wish you hadn't done
that."

"I was protecting myself from a stranger," he reminded her, echoing lessons she'd taught him, his
childlike voice carefully enunciating the grown-up
words.

Her son had bitten the man she was planning to
marry. She closed her eyes. Had she thought things

were slipping out of control? *Galloping* was more like it. She caught her breath and straightened her shoulders. There had to be a way to salvage the situation, but it had better be done quickly.

"Come on," she told Rusty, swinging him down to his feet. "Let's go into the other room. You have to apologize."

He hung back, dread filling his shining eyes. "Do I have ta?"

"Yes, you have ta. Come on. And make it sincere."

He slunk along beside her, trying to hide behind her skirt as they made their way into the living room, where the man he'd bitten was waiting.

Joe was still pondering the letter, his blue eyes frowning, but his expression changed as he looked up to see Chynna and Rusty coming toward him. His gaze narrowed appreciatively as he watched her neat form walking briskly through the room. No, it still didn't make sense. If you really could get something like this from a catalog, the mail would be swamped with orders. How did his brother get so lucky?

She stopped before him, tugging on her son's arm to pull him out from behind her. "Rusty tells me he bit you," she said, going right to the point. "He wants to apologize."

"Oh, yeah." He'd forgotten about that. He held out his hand and looked at it. The bite marks were still quite distinct, though the skin hadn't broken. Shrugging, he smiled at the freckle-faced boy. "This is nothing. Baby bites. You want to see where my brother bit me when he was about ten?" He pushed back his sleeve and revealed a long, jagged scar on his bicep. "Now, that's what I call a bite," he said rather proudly. "It tore flesh open. The traveling nurse had to be flown in to give me stitches."

Rusty stared at him with wide eyes, but if Joe had been harboring any thoughts of bringing the boy closer with his old war stories, he realized he wasn't going to win over the kid this way. Instead of laughing or looking impressed, Rusty looked terrified.

Joe looked into those pained eyes and shrugged. What the hell, he was no good with kids. Never had been. And there was hardly any point in getting close to a boy he was never going to see again after...

Now, that was just the point, he thought as he rolled his sleeve back down. After what? How long was he staying and how close a relationship were they going to be forced into? He glanced into Chynna's lovely face. It didn't tell him a thing.

"We need to talk," he said evenly.

She nodded. "Of course," she said crisply. "But I need to feed my children. They haven't had anything since midmorning. I'll fix something for all of us and put them down for a nap, and then we can go over the ground rules."

His mouth relaxed into a lopsided grin. Her phrasing struck him as amusing. "The ground rules?" he repeated. "I only want a discussion, not a sparring session."

She tossed her head back and gave him a cocky smile that didn't quite warm her eyes. "You may just get both," she told him as she turned away. "Be prepared."

He gave her a Boy Scout salute, but she didn't see it. She was already halfway out of the room, Rusty clinging to her and glancing back as though afraid Joe might be following them.

Watching him, seeing the apprehension in his eyes, Joe winced, thinking of how the boy would deal with Greg. His brother wasn't known for compassion or tact. In fact, he'd always considered him a sort of goofy recluse, sort of a mountain man with no need for real human companionship. To think of him ordering up a woman came as something of a shock. And knowing his brother, to have the woman show up with two kids in tow would not go over awfully well. She would be lucky to get out of here before Greg got back.

But where was Greg, anyway? Why wasn't he here to greet his bride-to-be?

Joe turned and gave the room another quick examination. The place was surprisingly clean, though there was clutter here and there. He'd noticed dishes in the sink, but the food hadn't been on them long. Two long strides brought him to the storage-room closet, and opening it, he discovered that his brother had taken camping gear and cooking equipment. If he'd left that morning, it looked as if he wouldn't be back for a few days.

Joe swore softly and shook his head. "In the meantime, what am I supposed to do with your girlfriend, you idiot?" he murmured.

But there was no reply that made any sense at all.

He heard Chynna's steps and turned to meet her as she came through the doorway into the hall.

"We're almost ready," she told him, looking cool and efficient. "I'd like to put them down for naps right after they eat. Which bedroom may I use?"

"Bedroom?" She was obviously planning to stay, and he was going to have to decide what he was prepared to do to get her back on a plane to wherever it was she'd said she came from. "Uh…let me take a look."

There were three bedrooms in the house. The large one his parents had used still held a four-poster double bed. Next to it was what his mother had always called the green room, a place set up specifically for guests, with the best bed and nicest furniture. He assumed the bedroom at the end of the hall, which he'd shared with Greg, was still set up with twin beds.

He looked into the master bedroom and gestured toward the old-fashioned bed. "They could sleep here," he said.

She looked around him and nodded. "That would be fine," she said quietly. "Now, where do I sleep?"

He opened his mouth to say something, then closed it again. Looking down, he met her gaze, and something in the spark he saw in her eyes set him back on his heels. After all, she thought he was Greg. She thought they were more or less engaged. Funny. He'd never been this close to matrimony before. It felt spooky, and he wasn't real clear on just what she expected of him.

There was only one way to find out. He would have to be blunt. "You're not thinking about doing any sleeping together or anything like that, are you?" he asked, trying for a light, humorous tone, but ending up glancing at her suspiciously.

She grinned at him, and in that moment, he knew he'd fallen in a trap and he'd been sucker punched. "Of course not," she said primly. "Not until we're married." She turned and led the way down the hall. "How about this room?" she asked, nudging open the door to the middle bedroom. "Who sleeps in here?"

"I guess you will," he told her grudgingly. "At

least for tonight. You might as well bring your things in.''

''Great.'' She smiled at him. ''I'll unpack as soon as we finish our meal.''

He wanted to point out that unpacking would be premature, but she made her way back toward the kitchen before he got the chance, and he shook his head instead, angry with himself for not making it clear right away.

''You're not staying here,'' he said aloud, but there was no one there to hear him.

Kids were weird. That was the conclusion Joe came to after sitting down to a meal with two of them. The little girl, Kimmie, as they seemed to call her, had a hard time eating, seeing as how she refused to take her thumb out of her mouth. And Rusty ate quickly, glancing up at Joe as though he were afraid the large man would grab his food right off his plate if he didn't watch him carefully. Chynna tried hard to get a pleasant conversation going, but it was no use. For that, they needed a certain level of comfort and trust that just wasn't there.

''The countryside around here certainly is beautiful,'' Chynna remarked. ''Flying in, you could almost see the curve of the earth. The forests look like they could go on forever.''

Joe grunted, but his attention was diverted by the sight of Rusty's chipmunk cheeks bulging with food. Was he expecting a long, hard winter? Or just making up for lost time? Hard to tell.

''I imagine you're snowed in here most of the winter,'' she went on. ''It doesn't look like snowplows would get out this way.''

"Uh...no," he muttered, distracted as Kimmie, thumb firmly in place in her mouth, picked up a pea with her spare hand and calmly smashed it against her nose. He grimaced and looked up at Chynna, wondering where she stood on the playing-with-your-food issue and why she wasn't doing something to stop the child.

"Should she...?" he began.

He gestured toward the little girl, but Chynna was already cleaning the smashed vegetable off her daughter's nose with a napkin, making the move as though it were something she did every day, and going right on.

"This is going to be a very different experience for us," she said serenely. "The children have always lived in the city. And come to think of it," she added with a quick smile, "so have I."

"What city was that?" he asked, just making conversation.

"Chicago."

"Oh. Nice lake." Not a particularly compelling comment, but he had an excuse. His attention was being distracted by the eating habits of children, things he'd never dreamed he would see at the table.

At this moment, Rusty was returning a mouthful of egg to the plate, looking as though he'd been poisoned. Joe stifled a groan, his appetite completely gone. Chynna deftly whipped away the disgusting plate and handed her son a glass of milk, not mentioning what had happened and cleaning up the evidence as quickly as possible.

"I notice you don't have a television," she said, wiping a newly smashed pea from Kimmie's nose and stopping the hand that reached to get another one.

Joe was just glad one hand was occupied with the thumb in the mouth. If the kid had both hands free, who knew what she might rub into her face. He glanced at her, his eyebrows drawn together in a look of bewildered horror. So this was what it was like to be around children? How wise he'd been to avoid it in the past.

But the woman had been asking him something— whether they had television, wasn't that it? "Uh…no, no television. No signal makes it out this far very effectively."

"That's just as well," she said. "Television is a major purveyor of exactly what I wanted to get them away from."

"No kidding." He threw down his napkin and glanced at the door, wondering if it would be rude to take a walk. A long, extended walk. Maybe go right past these kids' bedtime.

"We've brought along some music tapes the kids like to listen to. You do have a stereo, so they'll be able to use that."

"Children's songs," he muttered, hoping someone would warn him. He wanted to be out of the house before the chanting songs about beluga whales started up. He'd had a friend with a two-year-old once, and the sappy whale song he heard at their house still haunted his nightmares.

Chynna read the aversion in his face and she bit her lower lip, her dark eyes clouded in thought. This was turning out to be more difficult than she'd expected, but she wasn't going to let that get her down. She was used to coming up against brick walls and learning to dismantle them. Life had been like that for her so far. Not too many primrose paths in her background.

Plenty of thistles and thorns and rivers to cross. When you came from times like that, you got tough or you crumbled. Chynna had no intention at all of crumbling. She was going to end up married to this man. That was a promise.

But for some reason, the kids were not cooperating. She glanced at them with a sigh, and then her gaze lingered and her heart filled with sweet love for them. Poor babies. What did she expect? They'd been wrenched away from the only home they'd ever known, flown across the country for hours, shuttled off in the small plane and plunked down in a gloomy old house in the middle of nowhere. And here was their harried mother, demanding they be on their best behavior. No wonder they seemed ragged and stressed out.

Sleep. That was what they needed.

"There's no telephone," Joe said, and she looked up, startled.

No telephone. That was going to bother her, and she knew it. But then, she reminded herself, that was what she'd come out here for. Maybe it was too many modern conveniences that had turned life upside down in the city. She'd wanted the opposite of that, and if giving up the telephone would help her get it, who was she to quibble?

"We'll get used to it," she said firmly. There would be no ordering out for pizza. But there would also be no crank calls, no banks calling to sell their credit cards, nobody selling tickets for the policemen's ball. Life would go on.

"Nap time," she murmured, untying Kimmie's bib though she hadn't really swallowed a thing.

Kimmie stared up, her dark eyes huge as she gazed

around her fist at her mother, clinging to that thumb with all her might.

"I'm not sleepy," Rusty said fretfully, but he rubbed his eyes and yawned, and Chynna knew it was only a matter of time before his eyelids began to droop.

Softly, as she cleaned them up from their meal and began to shepherd them into the bedroom they would be using, she began to sing a lullaby.

"'Good night, say the teddy bears, it's time to close our eyes.'" She'd sung it to the two of them at bedtime since they were babies, and by now it worked like magic. They heard the gentle melody and they both relaxed, knowing it was time for a nap, knowing there was nothing that could keep sleep away. That was just the way it was.

Joe watched her with a frown. It was all very well that she was a wizard with her kids, but what did that mean in the long run? Greg and kids—no, the two concepts clashed like…like pickles and ice cream. It wouldn't work. He had to talk her into going back to Chicago, back to where she'd come from.

Rising, he began carrying dishes to the sink and tried to think of what he would use as his salient point. He was a lawyer, after all. All those years of training in logic and argument were finally going to come to something. No problem. Once he got going, she would be putty in his hands.

He rinsed off the dishes and stacked them, turning when he heard her coming back into the kitchen.

"They're down for their naps," she said simply, giving him a quick smile. "We can talk."

"Nice work," he said, complimenting her, his head tilted to the side as he looked her over. Nice work, he repeated silently to himself, but this time his comment was related to the state the woman was in herself. She still looked crisp and efficient in her blouse and skirt, but her hair had come undone just enough to leave wisps flying about her face in a very fetching way. She was one attractive woman.

"Shall we sit?" he offered, gesturing toward the chairs at the table.

She nodded and preceded him, glancing up in surprise when he helped her with her chair.

He took his place opposite her and narrowed his gaze, ready to lay down the law as he saw it.

"Let me see if I have this straight," he began. "You put yourself in a catalog for men who want mail-order brides. Greg answered, selected you and sent you money to come to Alaska. You brought along two kids you hadn't told him about, hoping he would take them as part of the bargain. But Greg wasn't here when you arrived. Is that about it?"

She stared at him for a moment, wondering how long he was going to try to keep up this pretense that he wasn't Greg. She was sure he was going to try to use it as an excuse to get out of their contract. He'd taken one look at the kids and panicked. That had to be it. Now he wanted to get rid of her so he could order himself up another woman, someone who would come unencumbered with little ones.

Well, she understood his angle. She'd been afraid something like this might happen. But she wasn't going to give up quite that easily. What she needed was time...time for him to get to know the children, time for him to get to know her and what kind of person she was. Once that happened, surely she would be able to talk him into taking them as a set. All she needed was time.

"That's about it," she said evenly. Leaning forward on her elbows, she decided to let him have his game without protest at this point. "The only part you left out was how committed I am to making this work out for all of us."

He gazed into her dark eyes and found only sincerity, but he couldn't hide his smile of skepticism.

"Hey," he said softly. "I didn't just fall off the turnip truck, you know. This doesn't make any sense, and you know it."

She raised one delicately molded eyebrow. "Do I?"

His short laugh said it all. "Sure. Look, Chynna, you're a beautiful woman. I can't believe you've ever had any problem getting a man." He turned his hand palm up on the table. "What would a woman like you need to resort to these measures for?"

For the first time, her gaze wavered. "I never claimed I had problems getting men," she retorted stiffly.

He shrugged as though that proved his case. "Then why did you do it? Why did you make this contract with my brother?"

She hesitated, her eyes cloudy. "I have my reasons," she said at last. "I'll explain it all to you at some point. But I'm not quite ready to open up on every private hope and dream I have. Not yet."

His mouth twisted as he studied her. "Why didn't you tell Greg about the kids?" he asked.

She wet her upper lip with a quick slip of her tongue. "I knew what your first reaction would be," she said simply. "I wanted you to get to know them before you turned them down."

"I'm not Greg," he said automatically, but he wasn't really thinking about that. He stared at her. Nothing she said added up. There had to be something else going on here. But what?

"Sorry. 'Joe,' isn't it?" she amended, rolling her eyes only slightly but letting the tone of her voice emphasize the way she felt about this masquerade she thought he was playing.

"'Joe' it is," he stated flatly. "Always has been and always will be. And Greg..." He hesitated, then leaned forward, determined to get this cleared up and out in the open once and for all. "Listen, Greg is my brother. I know him well. And believe me, he's not husband material in any sense of the word."

She lifted her chin and met his gaze steadily. She had to admit, she liked what she saw. His face was tan, with grooves where dimples had probably once been, and tiny laugh lines around his eyes. From what she'd seen so far, she would say he was a very nice guy, and one who seemed to see the humor in most things. A man like that should be ready to love children. Why wasn't it happening?

"Not husband material?" she repeated. "I see. What's wrong with him?"

He shrugged, feeling uncomfortable to be spilling family secrets. But in this case, he didn't see any alternative. "It's not that there is anything wrong with him, per se. It's just that he's..." He narrowed his eyes, trying to think of the right words. "He's a real Alaska guy, you know what I mean? If this were ninety years ago, he'd be digging for gold in the mountains. If this were a hundred and fifty years ago, he'd be living off the land, tromping around in snowshoes and only coming down to civilization once a year for supplies. This is not a man who is set up, either psychologically or emotionally, to take care of a family.''

"Oh?'' She narrowed her eyes, too, staring right back at him. "Then why did he pick me? Why did he send me the money to come join him?'' She picked up the envelope that was lying on the table between them and pulled out the photograph, dangling it from her fingers. "Why did he send me this picture of himself? And why did he say the things he did?'' She shrugged delicately. "Maybe you don't know him as well as you think you do,'' she suggested.

He frowned, watching her wave the picture around and feeling like punching his brother in the nose once he found him again. This would have been a lot simpler if Greg had sent a picture of himself instead of using Joe as bait. "I can't really explain why he did those things,'' he said shortly. "Maybe he was playing around with a dream and then got cold feet when it looked as though it might actually come true.''

She snapped the photo back into the envelope. "Yes, that's the thing, isn't it?'' she said sweetly. "This has come true. Here we are. So let's make the best of it.'' She rose, starting toward the kitchen sink, but he stopped her with a hand on her arm.

"Listen, you don't seem to get it. I think you should pack up your kids and get while the getting's good. Leave. Take a plane and head out. Go back to where you came from.''

Staring down at him, she slowly shook her head. "The pilot of the little plane that brought us from Anchorage said he wouldn't be back this way for four days,'' she noted. "We can't leave, even if we wanted to.''

He swallowed hard. This was a reminder of what it was like to live out in the boonies. That just showed how quickly one could get used to modern life in a big city, where every convenience was at beck and call at any moment of the day or night.

"Oh," he said, letting his hand drop. "Well, I suppose I could drive you to Anchorage."

The lack of enthusiasm for that idea was evident in his voice, and she smiled suddenly, shaking her head again. "Don't bother," she said crisply, turning back toward the sink. "We'll stay. You need us."

"Like a hole in the head," he muttered to himself as he made his way toward the front door. There was only one thing left to do. He had to find his brother, or at least find out where he was and when he was planning to drop in on this hardy little band of squatters who had taken over his house.

"Where are you going?" she called after him, leaning out of the kitchen door.

He looked back at her. "I'm going to see if I can find out where Greg went."

He expected to see a flash of annoyance in her eyes, but instead he saw a flare of fear. "You are coming back, aren't you?" she called.

"Of course I'm coming back."

He turned toward the car, not wanting to see her face, see the questions in her eyes. She still thought he was pretending not to be Greg. Well, it hardly mattered. She probably thought he was a little nuts, but then, if she were confronted with the real Greg, she would do more than think it.

And yet, that was hardly fair. He hadn't seen his brother for a number of years. It was possible he'd turned into a model citizen after all. Yes, it was possible. Just barely.

He swung behind the wheel of the long, low sports car he'd rented in Anchorage and started the engine, thinking how out of place a car like this was out here in the wilderness.

"And that's exactly why I love it," he murmured, avoiding a pothole and turning onto the two-lane dirt road that would take him to the combination post office and general store that served as the center of Dunmovin, the so-called town he'd been born in thirty-some years before.

Three

The place looked the same, only a decade and a half older and more run-down. Right next to it was a shiny new building. The sign in the window said Nails By Nancy, and Joe stopped for a moment and stared at the little yellow storefront, wondering who in the world there was for Nancy to do the nails of—whoever Nancy was. Shaking his head, he took the steps into the general store two at a time and burst in through the front door.

The theme inside was pure familiarity. Goods were still stocked to the ceiling, stacked precariously on long plank shelves. A lazy fan took a fainthearted pass at stirring the air. Two ancient residents sat on chairs tilted back until they leaned against the wall, and Annie Andrews stood behind the counter, working on her account books.

She looked up over her glasses when she heard him

come in and gave a snort of surprise as he walked into the dusty little building.

"As I live and breathe. Joey Camden." The gray-haired woman folded her arms across her chest and gazed at him instead of giving him a hug, but her snapping black eyes and crooked grin were filled with the warmth of her welcome, and he appreciated it, grinning right back. "What brings you to these parts, stranger?"

"The call of the wild, I guess," he said, hooking his thumbs in his belt loops and rocking back on his heels. "You always told me Alaska would call me back."

She nodded, looking pleased. "That I did. And I'm always right, aren't I?"

"Always," he agreed. He glanced at the two old-timers, but though they were eagerly hanging on to every word of this conversation, he could see that he didn't know either one of them. He gave them a nod and turned back to Annie.

"You going to be living with your brother in that old house?" she asked him, her eyes sparkling at the thought of it.

He hesitated. "No, not exactly. In fact, I'm just here for a short visit. I'm on my way to see Mom."

Annie nodded, taking a swipe at the counter with a rag. "How is your mother?" she asked. "She writes me every year at Christmas, but it isn't the same as having her a mile or so down the road. She was one of the few females I ever got on well with around here."

"She's okay. Not as young as she used to be, and she's worrying me a bit." He moved awkwardly, not used to unburdening his soul, but somehow the truth came pouring out. Maybe it was because he was talking to a woman who had known him since he was a baby.

"Actually, that's why I came. I've been trying to get Greg to come into Anchorage and see her. But you know how he is. Cities give him hives. Or so he says."

"Unlike you, who loves them."

He shrugged and gave her a crooked grin. "You know me well, Miss Annie."

Annie nodded her appreciation for his use of the old term he'd used for her when he was a boy, but her brow furled. "Joey Camden, you're Alaska born and bred," she accused. "How can you stay down in that forsaken place in California when you know you should be back here where you belong?"

"Here?" He shook his head and laughed shortly. "Oh, no. I don't belong here anymore. I'm a city lawyer now, Annie. You remember. That's what I always wanted."

She nodded, looking a bit sulky. "Oh, yes, I remember it well. Bright lights and big cities, that was what you always said. And I always told you it wouldn't satisfy you for long."

"Well, that may just have been the one thing you were wrong about."

She shook her head, stubborn as ever. "Nope. I'm never wrong about things that have to do with the heart. You're the one who just hasn't woken up and smelled the coffee yet."

It certainly wasn't worth arguing about. "Maybe you're right," he allowed. "I see this town is going great guns. You've even got yourselves a nail parlor. How'd you get so lucky?"

Annie grinned. "Nancy came about a year ago.

Calls herself an eco-feminist. Wanted to hunt and fish and live as one with nature. You know the type. Wouldn't know nature if it came up and bit her where the sun don't shine.'' She chuckled, enjoying her own little joke. ''Turned out she was a total failure at the hunting-and-fishing stuff. Guns scared her, and she couldn't look a trout in the eye. Thought they were slimy. But I got to hand it to her—she wouldn't give up. I suppose partly it was that she didn't want to go back and face her eco-feminist friends with failure. Anyway, she decided she would stay, but go with avenues down which her talents really lie.''

''Nails,'' Joe guessed.

''Yup. And manicures for the guys, things like that.''

''Oh, come on, Annie. How many men around here want manicures?''

''Every dang one of them when the place first opened. You should have seen them. They were standing in line.''

Joe looked shocked, then his face changed as the light dawned. ''Oh. She's a looker, is she?''

Annie grinned. ''She's about the prettiest girl we've had around these parts since the Babbitt twins left for summer jobs at Disney World and never came back.''

Joe nodded. The twins had been about five years older than he, but he remembered well the sad day they left for the lower states. The men in Dunmovin had mourned for months.

''Anyway, that's neither here nor there. Let me fix you some dinner. How about it?''

He smiled. ''Thanks, Annie. But right now, I've got other things on my mind.'' He glanced around the little room again. "Do you have any idea where I could find my brother?"

Annie pursed her lips thoughtfully. "I take it you've already been out to the house," she began, then her eyes brightened. "Say, wait a minute. Billy McGee was in here earlier and he said some woman had come in on the mail plane, come to see Greg. Had two little kids with her."

Joe nodded. "That's right."

Her black eyes narrowed craftily. "Said she was coming here to marry Greg. Any truth in that?"

Joe hesitated, then shrugged. "I'm not sure about that."

Annie leaned forward and pinned him with her flashing gaze. "Said she was some sort of mail-order bride. Any truth in that?"

Joe sighed and gave her a long, lazy look. This was not a rumor he wanted spread. "I thought mail-order brides went out when the gold fields dried up," he said silkily. "I never did believe a woman would do something like that, anyway."

Annie snorted. "I know plenty of men who would jump at the chance to pick out a wife like they pick out their drill presses and their Sunday-go-to-meetin' clothes. Just choose a number and send in a check and she's yours, for better or for worse."

"Mostly worse, likely."

Annie raised an eyebrow. "Who knows? The divorce rate ain't so great on matches people choose for themselves when they supposedly fall in love first."

He grinned at her. "You've got a point there." His grin faded and he grimaced, leaning closer so that only Annie could hear him. "Tell you the truth, she does

claim she's here because Greg...well, because he sent
for her. You don't know anything about this?''

Annie's eyes glittered but she shook her head. ''No,
really. Greg has never been one to whisper his secrets
in my ear.''

Joe grinned. ''I know that. I just thought you might
have noticed the mail going back and forth.''

One eyebrow rose. ''Now that you mention it, there
was a lot of correspondence there for a while. You
know, Greg comes in with his bills once a month.
That's usually the only time I ever see him. Oh, and
when the *Field and Stream* magazines come in, he's
always here the next day. But he was coming in almost
every other day for a while.'' She gasped. ''Wait a
minute. I do seem to remember overhearing him talk
about some girl he was going to get hitched with. I
didn't pay it much mind—you know how your brother
tends to...'' She hesitated.

''Lie?'' Joe supplied.

''Well, now, I wouldn't go so far as to say that.
How about he just embroiders the truth a little? He
likes to make life dramatic.''

''Yeah, right.'' Joe nodded, his mouth twisting cyn-
ically. ''Meanwhile...I've got a bride on my hands,
and no groom in sight. If you see Greg, tell him to get
his tail on home and clean up this mess.''

''You can bet I'll do exactly that.'' She followed
him to the door of the building and added gruffly,
''And you come on back and see me again before you
leave. You hear?''

''Will do.'' Surprising her, surprising even himself,
he bent down and dropped a quick kiss on her cheek.
''See you later, Miss Annie.''

She pressed her hand to where he'd made his imprint and colored as he left, swinging down the steps and sliding behind the wheel of his fancy car. "You always were a little dickens," she muttered, but she couldn't hold back the pleased smile, and she shook her head as he waved, taking off in a dust cloud.

It was eerie walking into the house and hearing someone in the kitchen. Almost like the old days. But it was even eerier hearing children playing in the living room. That wasn't much like old days. Joe and his brother never played happily like Rusty and Kim were doing. They had mainly fought.

Joe stopped in the doorway, watching the kids. They'd rigged up an old sheet between two armchairs and were using it as a tent. Kim was under the canopy, sitting cross-legged, swaying and singing a song to herself. Rusty was being an airplane, zooming around the room, stopping to babble something unintelligible at the two long-tailed goldfish who were swimming lazy laps in their bowl on the hutch, then turning abruptly to swoop toward Kim, making her shriek with delighted fear. For a moment, Joe took in the play and wondered at it. So this was what happy children did. He realized he didn't know much about kids, when you came right down to it. All he knew about was the way he and his brother had been, and the word *happy* hadn't come up much.

Suddenly, Rusty caught sight of him and stopped dead. Kim whirled, saw him and her thumb went straight into her mouth.

"Hi, kids," he said, feeling a little awkward.

They stayed still as statues, staring at him, as though they had to be prepared to run if he took another step toward them.

He searched his mind for a topic of conversation, but came up with nothing. Then his gaze fell on the goldfish bowl.

"Hey, how do you like these two guys?" he asked heartily. "Aren't they cute?"

Rusty looked at the bowl and nodded. "What are their names?" he asked.

"Uh…" How should he know? But pets had to have names. "Goldie and Piranha," he said off the top of his head. "Do you like goldfish?"

Neither of them said anything. Both just stared at him, and he found himself sweating under this kind of scrutiny. Swearing softly under his breath, he turned away. Obviously, he had no natural knack with children. That was hardly surprising. Still, it hurt a little to think kids hated him on sight.

On the other hand, women usually liked him just fine, and there happened to be one on the premises. Feeling better about it all, he made his way to the kitchen, where he'd heard those busy sounds when he'd first come back into the house.

Chynna was at the sink and he stopped, startled by the change. She'd cast off her business suit for jeans and a jersey top that hugged her curves like—well, it might be best not to go on with that simile. And it might be important not to let his gaze linger too long on the more spectacular elements. Shifting his attention to the dishwater, he came in and plunked himself down at the table.

"How did you know," he asked abruptly, "that you were going to like kids? Before you had them, I mean. What gave you the courage to take the plunge?"

She looked at him for a moment, turning her head so that her long, loose hair swung like a pendulum at her back, and laughed. "What did they do to you now?" she asked, one hand on her hip.

He managed an innocent look. "Nothing. Not a thing." Then his conscience got the better of him. "Well, if they were a little older, I'd say they snubbed me. But since they're just kids..."

"Kids can break your heart, too," she said softly. "They're so open and innocent about it. They haven't learned to hide their feelings, so what they do comes straight from their soul. That can hurt a lot."

"Yeah." He shrugged it off. "I guess you're just a natural with children, aren't you?"

She threw back her head and laughed, surprising him. "Hardly," she said, her eyes dancing with amusement. "I made a lot of mistakes. I still make them."

He shook his head. "It's all too complex for me. I don't think I'll ever have kids. I have enough trouble keeping a dog happy."

The laughter evaporated from her face like spring rain on hot pavement. This was not the way she wanted things to go.

"Kids are great," she said quickly. "They grow on you."

"Like fungus?" He made a face. "No, thanks. I think I'll pass."

"You'll see," she said, gazing at him seriously. "You'll see."

He looked back into her deep, dark eyes, and something he saw there—or maybe something he didn't see—made him uneasy.

"Listen," he began, feeling as though he had to explain things to her, make her face the fact that he wasn't Greg, that he would never go for kids, that he doubted if Greg would, either, that she had made a big mistake coming here to Alaska.

But as though she read his mind and didn't want to hear it, she turned away, reaching for the pan she'd been scouring, and the words stopped in his throat. At the same time, he noticed she'd been cleaning.

"Wow," he said, examining the kitchen, first one side and then the other. The tile on the counters was shining, and the boxes of food that had been stacked there earlier had vanished. "You didn't need to do this."

She laughed again, more softly this time. "Let's put it this way—it needed to be done."

He shook his head in wonder. Even the old cookie jar was glistening. "I've never seen this place look so good."

"Really?" She turned back, pleased. "I've only just begun."

That caught him up short. He rose and came toward her, frowning. "No, listen. You shouldn't be doing this. This isn't your job. You're a visitor and..."

She put a hand up to stop his speech. "I'm no visitor," she told him calmly. "I told you. I'm applying for a job." She tried a fetching smile. "I'm going to make myself indispensable to you."

"Indispensable," he murmured, repeating her word in a bit of a daze. The concept was overwhelming, and he found himself backing out of the kitchen, not sure what to do or what to say.

He muttered something, and she turned back to the sink. After a last, lingering look, he left, but the effect she had stayed with him. He felt very strange. The thought of a woman like this fighting for a place in his heart—but wait. That was pure bull. This had noth-

ing to do with him, per se. She wasn't trying to win
him over. She thought she was working to win over
Greg. And in the end, Greg's decision was the one
that was going to count. What Joe thought wouldn't
mean anything to anyone.

Feeling oddly resentful, restless and out of place, he
sauntered into the hallway and then, slowly, made his
way into the bedroom he'd shared with his brother for
all the years of his childhood. Once again, the past hit
him between the eyes.

"God, Greg," he muttered, gazing at the room.
"Don't you ever throw anything away?"

The same old madras spreads lay on the twin beds.
The same old rocking chair stood in the corner. His
dusty old L.A. Lakers poster still hung over his bed,
with Kareem Abdul Jabar stretching his long, long
body toward the basket. And there was his basketball,
looking like a partially deflated balloon, sitting on his
old dresser.

He glanced at Greg's side of the room. Greg had
mounted a collection of arrowheads in a case during
his last year of high school, and it still stood against
the wall. The only thing different was a stack of com-
pact discs and a small disc player on the nightstand.
And there, next to the disc player, was a catalog. A
catalog of women who wanted husbands.

Joe let his breath out in a long sigh as he grabbed
the book and brought it to his side of the room, sinking
down to sit on the edge of his old bed. This was it.
Shopping for wives. Very gingerly, he cracked open
the catalog and began to peruse it, feeling a strange
sense of reluctance, but unable to stop.

He gazed at the pictures as he flipped through the
book, studying the faces. Some looked half witted.

Many looked scared or desperate. The faces from war-torn or poverty-stricken countries looked tight, deter-mined, eager to escape their situations and try life in the land of the free. He could see why they might be ready to trade independence for a better life. That was understandable. But why would a woman like Chynna, a normal woman from Chicago—what reason could she possibly have? It didn't make any sense.

And then he found her picture. She looked natural, but just a little reserved. There was a cool, self-possessed sense to her pose, to the look in her eyes, the tilt of her chin. And she looked damn beautiful.

Wow, he thought, frowning. It would take a brave and self-confident man to order up a woman like this. She looked like a handful, even in the picture she'd sent to sell herself with. It was hard for him to imagine Greg gathering that sort of courage.

But then again, maybe that was why he'd cleared out before she got here.

"He probably got drunk, wrote the letter and sent her a check, and then suffered buyer's remorse the very next day," he decided. "And was too chicken to call her and cancel."

The thought of it made him grin. Yes, that was what probably had happened. Which meant he was going to have to tell her, and watch those huge brown eyes cloud up.

His grin began to fade. "Thanks a lot, Greg," he muttered, closing the catalog and staring out the win-dow at the pines. "Thanks a hell of a lot."

Chynna plunged her hands into the tepid dishwater and tried to make her mind go blank while she soaped down the parts of the ancient stove she'd just disconnected. There was something satisfying about scrubbing everything clean.

"It's another form of renewal," she told herself. Besides, it helped her keep her mind off things.

She frowned, trying hard to concentrate on making charred porcelain shine again, but the thoughts kept coming anyway. How could she help but think about it? It was here, it was now and it had to be dealt with.

She stopped and took a deep breath, letting her mind go, letting the thoughts flow in.

"Okay," she whispered to herself. "Here's the deal." She had to make the man fall in love with her.

That was the crux of the matter, and it chilled her blood. She'd never had a lack of male attention. Wherever she went, men tended to let her know by looks or actions that they liked what they saw when they looked at her. But those things had never ranked highly in her list of important reasons she'd been put on this earth. In fact, her good looks were often more a nuisance than a benefit to her. She'd always had a more serious bent, with goals and a good, strong work ethic. She had never had any interest in being a playgirl. And because she never played, she'd never been very good at flirting. She didn't think she could manage a coy look if her life depended on it.

"But it does," she whispered to herself, biting her lip. Her life and the lives of her two babies depended on it.

Shaking her head, she went back to scrubbing, but her mind was in turmoil. Greg was acting very strangely. And instead of meeting that fact head-on, she was washing things.

"That's because you didn't prepare properly," she

scolded herself. "And now you don't know what to do next."

That was it. She needed time to regroup. This situation wasn't really turning out the way she'd pictured it would. She'd expected awkwardness at first, sure. After all, how did one act around a man one planned to marry when one had never had a real conversation with him before? They were tied together in the most serious way a man and woman could be tied, and yet they were virtual strangers. Intimacy was going to take time. That was only natural.

But did she have time? She wasn't sure. That was the problem. He wasn't acting as though he wanted her to stay.

And that was why she was going to have to make him fall in love. "Either with me or the kids," she told herself. But she knew it was going to have to be with her. She was going to have to make herself irresistible. She rolled her eyes and pulled the plug on the dishwater, watching it spiral down the drain.

At least she seemed to have made a pretty darn good choice. All you had to do was look at him. He was wonderful, really. When she thought of the sort of man she could have ended up with, this seemed almost a miracle. She'd taken a big gamble and she'd been prepared to put up with some borderline cases to get what she needed for her children. And in that way, at least, her gamble had paid off handsomely. He was a catch.

That didn't mean things looked rosy. Hardly that. He was still leery, still pretending not to be Greg. And he hadn't warmed to the children. That was going to take time. But it would come. It had to. Her kids were adorable. Everyone said so. They were just a little shy of him right now. Tomorrow would be different.

Tomorrow. She would clean like crazy, cook something unforgettable, show off her great kids and he wouldn't be able to resist. She would have him in wedding clothes by the end of the week.

"It's got to work," she muttered aloud as she dried her hands. "It's got to."

Evening was deepening into night, though the sky outside was light as ever, and there was no sign of Greg. Joe was beginning to think his conjecture was right. Greg had no intention of coming back while Chynna was here.

He threw down the outdoorsman magazine he'd been reading and ran a hand through his thick black hair. He pretended to be looking out at the wind in the treetops, but all the while, he was looking at her, across the room with her children. She was pretty hard to ignore.

It seemed she was always moving. When a shaft of sunlight caught her hair, it glowed gold and silver, and her hands with their long, slender fingers seemed to flutter around her children. She reminded him of some mythical goddess, half animal, half human.

"A swan," he breathed to himself at one point as she hovered over Rusty, helping him find a place in his book. "A big, beautiful swan, protecting her children."

Like *Swan Lake*.

Ballet?

He blinked, startled. He was thinking about ballet? Good Lord, what was happening to his mind? He'd only been to the ballet once. Glee, a girl he'd been dating in L.A., had dragged him to the Greek Theater to see people leap around on creaky boards in tights and tutus. The men seemed to be impersonating forest elves, and the women looked as if they were wearing Frisbees around their middles and could easily have been launched into space at any moment. The music had been nice, but the dancing had not thrilled him.

"Don't take it all so literally," Glee had chided him when he grumbled. "Let go. Watch the movements. Feel the emotions."

Feeling emotions was not a well-loved hobby of his. He'd never thought much of feelings. As far as he was concerned, emotions were something to avoid, something to tamp down into a little corner of your soul and take out again only when you were alone and had time to deal with them. Emotions were not to be set prancing out on a stage on tiptoes for all to see. Emotions were things that couldn't always be avoided—but then, so were bad head colds. And he didn't like either one of them.

He was going to have to get her to leave in the morning. Did she realize that yet? Once she was gone, Greg would straggle back in from wherever he was hiding and Joe could get the job done he'd come to take care of. That was the only logical sequence of events. She was going to have to listen to reason. Maybe it would be best to get things settled tonight.

Looking up, she caught his gaze on her and she gave him a quick smile. "Is it ever going to get dark?" she wondered. "It's almost nine, and outside it looks like late afternoon."

"It's worse in late June," he told her. "There will be weeks when it never gets dark at all."

"Never gets dark," she repeated, shaking her head. "How do you convince children it's time to go to bed?"

He glanced at her kids and smiled. "My mother used to tell us if we closed our eyes, we could make it dark in our own heads and we wouldn't know the difference."

She laughed. "And that worked?"

"No. But we pretended it did so she wouldn't feel bad."

Rusty said something, and she turned her attention back to the children, but Joe couldn't stop watching her. Just being in this house was conjuring up memories he hadn't let surface in years. But having her here was something else altogether. Her presence called up thoughts and feelings he had no intention of setting free—things he had no right to think about.

So he wouldn't. But he wasn't going to worry about it. After all, she would be gone by this time tomorrow. All he had to do was find her and her kids a ride with someone driving into Anchorage. That was the ticket.

He watched as she got her children to put away their things and start preparing for bed, gathering them together, coaxing them on. And on the way to the bedroom, she marched them past him.

"Say good-night to Mr. Camden, children," she told them.

"'Night, Mr. Camden," Rusty said, staring down at his chunky green tennis shoes.

"Good night, kids," he replied a little too heartily.

Kimmie said nothing. Her thumb was jammed tightly into her mouth, and no sounds could squeeze out around it.

Chynna sighed with resignation and dragged them on into the bedroom, talking to them softly as she went. Listening, Joe sank back into his chair. In a moment, what he'd been hoping for happened and he smiled. She'd begun to sing to them again. Her voice was light, vaguely sensual, and it had magic in it. As he listened, his muscles dissolved and he slowly melted into the armchair, his head falling back, his eyes closed.

The next thing he knew, she was touching his shoulder.

"What?" He straightened quickly, blinking away sleep. "What happened?"

Her eyes were huge, and she was leaning close. "There's something outside," she whispered, obviously alarmed. "Listen."

He listened, but he didn't hear a thing. Glancing at her, he frowned, embarrassed to have fallen asleep. A look at the clock told him he'd been out for half an hour. Probably his snoring was what she'd heard.

Her hand grabbed his upper arm at the same time he heard it—a low, mournful sound coming from behind the house.

"There it is," she said quickly, her fingers tightening on his biceps. "What was that?"

He liked the feel of her hand on him, and in his groggy state, he wasn't resisting her attractions as well as he should. An urge swept over him, something that involved grabbing and pulling her down on the chair in his lap, but luckily he was awake enough to resist it.

"It sounded like a wolf," he told her, though he was hardly paying any attention to the noise that had her galvanized. His gaze was on her face, her deep, dark eyes, the way wisps of hair flew about her face and framed it like a picture of pure beauty.

"Funny," he added vaguely, captivated by her closeness, but still trying to respond to her nervousness about the wolves. "They don't usually come out this way."

She nodded, though she could hardly have known that, and her nervous clutch on his arm didn't loosen. "A wolf? Right out there in the backyard?"

He looked at her more closely. "Sure. You knew there would be animals, didn't you? You knew there would be predators. Bears and cougars and wolves and foxes." That was it—scare her. Tell her she couldn't avoid animals that would tear her and her children from limb to limb. Then maybe she would be happy to leave in the morning.

But he didn't want to lay it on too thick, and he found himself sticking to the truth, the way he usually did. "We're camped on the edge of the wilderness, you know. We share the land with animals of all kinds."

She swallowed hard and nodded again. Of course she knew. How could she not know? She was rational, educated, thinking—and completely shaken by this contact with the wild. It was one thing to think about animals in the woods; it was another to hear a wolf howl and realize there was something new she was going to have to protect her children from.

She turned from him, taking air deep into her lungs and steadying herself. She'd been so anxious to get away from the predators of the city, she'd forgotten there would be dangerous species out here, as well. Trying to raise two children on her own, she could afford only neighborhoods that were much too often filled with gangs and shootings and robberies. That was why she'd brought her children to this clean, pure wilderness. She should have remembered that there were dangers everywhere. They varied in type and style, but they had to be dealt with and vanquished, no matter where you went.

She would learn. Her children would learn. Greg would teach them. She looked at him, at his wide shoulders, his clear eyes, and she congratulated herself once again. Yes, he'd been the right pick. Of all the men who had contacted her when her ad came out in the catalog, he'd been the one she chose, and she'd done well. She had all the confidence in the world in him. And anyway, what choice did she have at this point?

"It's just going to take a little getting used to," she told him, managing a quick smile. "Do they...do they keep it up all night?"

"No. They'll be moving on, looking for something to kill."

Her face registered shock, and he swore softly, kicking himself for putting it like that. "I didn't mean that the way..."

She shook her head quickly, stopping his apology in its tracks. "No, I understand. That's the way it is out here, and we've got to adjust to it. I guess we're used to a life that's several layers away from nature and we forget how things really are."

How things really are. Her words echoed in his head as he watched her walk away from him, on her way to the green room, where she would sleep for the night. The wolf howled again, a little farther away this time, and Joe's head rose, almost as though his instinct was to catch a scent in the wind, and a shiver ran through him. God, he'd missed that sound, the wild passion, the sense of the conqueror. The call of nature was strong in him for a moment. After all, he'd grown up here; he'd been bound to this land and its animals from birth. He couldn't very well erase that, even if he wanted to. And right now, with the sound of the wolf still hanging in the air, he didn't want to. For the first time in years, he was remembering how much he loved it.

Four

Joe couldn't sleep. He must have had an hour or so before he woke, but then he couldn't drift off again, no matter how hard he tried, no matter how many sheep he counted or muscles he forced to relax. Finally, he gave up, rolling out of bed and pulling on his jeans and a sweater and going out into the pale twilight night to find some space to breathe in.

The old, familiar sounds washed over him, the whirring of insects, the scuffling of small animals underfoot, the flutter of an owl's wings as it swept past him, the roar of the river in the distance. The atmosphere was very different from the quiet suburban street in Los Angeles where traffic was the main noise, along with your neighbor's stereo system. He turned to look at the mountains, the snowy peaks shining iridescent in the night, and even as the thrill of it caught at his heart, he laughed softly.

"Damn you," he whispered. "Alaska, you old temptress. You're not going to seduce me. I'm too old and too strong to fall for this stuff."

But she was good. The very best. If he stayed too long…

But he wasn't going to do that. He was going to find his brother and force him to come visit his mother in Anchorage. That was what he'd come for, and he wouldn't leave until he'd done it. He owed his mother that much—and so did Greg. Of course, he was also going to have to take care of this new situation that was complicating things.

Turning, he looked toward the forest and stared for a moment, looking for movement.

"I know you're out there, Greg," he said aloud. "I'll bet you're not even very far away. And you're going to have to come in sometime. You're going to have to deal with this situation that you've set up. Come on, chicken. Come on in and face the music."

Greg didn't answer, though Joe waited a few minutes, wondering. Finally, he turned back toward the house and at the same time, saw a light go on in the master bedroom.

He stopped, frozen, as he watched Chynna enter the room and hover over her children, her white robe flowing around her like a cape. He could see her through the bedroom window, bending over her son, soothing him, a silhouette portrait of motherly love.

That was something he could admire from afar, but he was as sure as death that he could never feel that way about a kid. Never would happen. Not only did kids not warm to him, but the fatherly spirit just wouldn't gel in him. The question was, what made her think Greg was capable of it?

Still, he was the one watching this all through the window. And instead of turning away, as he knew he should, he stood and watched, mesmerized. She still bent over Rusty, whispering something to him, then she leaned closer to kiss the top of his head. Rising, she let her fingers trail across him as she looked over at Kimmie with a faint smile. At the doorway, she threw a kiss back to her boy, then turned off the light and shut the door.

Something about the entire scene got to him, touched him deeply in a way he didn't understand at all. Still standing in the same spot, Joe felt an ache grow in his chest, a yearning. He shook his head, shaking it away. He didn't need any of that. But he did need to get some things clear and he might as well take this opportunity to do it. He went quickly to the back door, catching Chynna before she made it back to her bedroom.

"Chynna. Can you come on out here for a minute?" he called to her softly. "I've got to get something off my chest."

She turned, startled, but came willingly enough, stepping out on the back porch and looking apprehensively toward the trees. "Are the wolves still around?" she asked, trying to keep her fear out of her voice.

"The wolves?" He'd forgotten all about them. "Oh, no. They're long gone."

Looking relieved, she came down the steps and joined him on the grass. "It's still so light," she said, marveling at the blue gray midnight sky. "Like a full-moon night. But there's no moon at all."

"The sun's down—it's just not very far away," he said, strolling toward the old wishing well his father had built in the back many years ago. But he was looking at the sky, as well. All his years in L.A. had made him forget how eerie it was, and at the same time, how wonderful.

She followed him, not saying a word, seemingly caught up in some of the same feelings. The night was huge. It seemed to stretch to forever. There was definitely a certain magic in the air.

He dropped to sit on a little stone bench near the well, and when he made room for her, Chynna sat beside him, pulling her robe in tight around her, and he immediately regretted having let her come so close. Her hair tumbled about her shoulders, and he could smell her scent, something light and fresh that tickled his nose. The sensuality of her swept over him, and he clenched his jaw, willing himself to ignore it. She turned toward him, and he steeled himself to meet her gaze.

"Where are your dogs?" she asked, surprising him.

"My what?"

"Your dogs. There are dog dishes on the floor in the kitchen. There's dog food in the cupboard. That doesn't usually happen without dogs. So where are they?"

"Dogs." He laughed shortly. "You're right. There are always at least two dogs around. Greg must have taken them with him."

Sighing, she looked toward the snowy mountains. "Whatever you say," she murmured.

She still thought he was Greg and trying to hide it. He grimaced. This was getting old. It was time she faced the truth.

"Listen, Chynna," he said briskly, looking up at the deep sky, "you're a very nice woman. And your kids are, well, they're okay. But you're going to have to leave tomorrow. There's no alternative.''

He didn't look at her, but he could feel her stiffen. He didn't want to see her face so he kept staring into the blue.

"Don't take it personally. This isn't your fault in any way. It's Greg's. I don't know what game he thought he was playing when he sent for you. But it's pretty obvious he isn't willing to keep his side of the bargain. And to tell you the truth, you're better off this way.''

"I don't agree," she said softly.

He glanced at her. Her voice was quiet, but there was a hint of steel in it. She wasn't going to give up easily. He was going to have to convince her to go.

"Listen, you really don't know what Greg is like," he began, wanting to explain the unexplainable.

"Don't I?" She broke in, sounding just a bit sarcastic. "Why don't you tell me all about him?"

He glanced at her set face, then looked away again. "I know this is hard to take, and I know you don't want to hear it, but I think you'd better know the truth. I have no idea why Greg put you to all this trouble, coming out here, and then taking off the way he did. But that's Greg. It's not really all that strange that he would act like that. In fact, it pretty much fits his character. He's always been moody, erratic, hard to handle. He'll go off for days at a time in the wilderness, just like he's doing now." He shrugged, wishing he was better with words to make this clear. "He's meant for this land and he'll never leave it.''

"Who said I ever wanted to leave it?"

He finally turned and met her gaze full on. "You

may not think so now, but you will. Women always do.''

She frowned. "Are you saying women can't handle this wild sort of country the way men can?" she demanded.

"That's exactly what I'm saying. Chynna, I grew up out here. I've seen it happen again and again. You don't know a thing about it." He shook his head. "But that's not really the point. We're not talking about women in general. We're talking about you." He gave her a baleful look, struck by the way she'd come out so defensively in support of women and their ability to handle the outdoor life. "What are you, some kind of feminist or something?"

She didn't rise to the bait. Instead, she stared at him for a long moment, then lifted her chin. "You just watch," she told him. "I know I can make it out here. I know I can."

There was plenty of determination in her voice, but he knew darn well she had no idea what she was talking about.

"Look, I know your heart's in the right place," he told her. "You mean well. But the wilderness will wear you down. You haven't lived here. You don't know. I've seen it happen so many times. Practically every man who brings a woman out here ends up alone in the long run. It's just the way things are."

The breeze blew a lock of her silvery hair across her eyes, and he had to hold back the urge to reach out and brush it back. She left it, let it fly, and his hand ached to touch her. Taking a deep breath, he forced himself to focus.

"Women like nice things. They like concerts and going out to dinner and dancing and shopping in nice stores. You can't do any of that out here. That sort of living might as well exist on another planet.''

He didn't see it coming or he would have prevented it, headed her off at the pass. But she moved quickly and before he knew it, she had his hand in hers, her fingers laced through his, and she was looking up earnestly, as though her heart were in her eyes.

"Greg, please listen. I've spent all my life in the city. I've gone to fancy restaurants and seen plays and taken college classes. I know what that is like. I've purposely turned my back on all of it. I wanted to come out here where things are clean and free. This is what I need. This is what my children need. Let us stay. You won't be sorry. I promise.''

Her hand burned on his, and her eyes were huge in the dim light. He wasn't a man to cave in, but this was some heavy artillery she was aiming his way. "Chynna…'' he began, but he wasn't sure where he was going with it.

It didn't matter. She had her own plans.

"Hold still,'' she told him, her voice firm but softly husky, and suddenly her free hand was pressed against his cheek. "I think we need something like this about now,'' she murmured, and stretching up, she touched his cool lips with her own.

A kiss. He hadn't expected it, but once it began, he knew it was something he had longed for from the moment he first saw her. He fell like a ton of bricks. All his good intentions evaporated into thin air. She took over his senses, all sweet tastes, soft touch and intoxicating scent. She went to his head like a shot of brandy, and he didn't even try to stop it. He accepted the kiss, letting her lips press to his for a moment, then, catching a sharp breath in his throat, he reached out and pulled her to him, taking her mouth as though he'd found a continent to conquer and meant to make quick work of it.

She melted to his touch, her bones seeming to disappear as she molded herself to him. Her mouth was sleek and plush, and he sank into it as though it would heal something in him if he only could go deeply enough. The male in him came alive and wanted her, right now, right there, and for a moment, he thought he felt an answering hunger from her. But then he could feel her drawing back, pulling away, and he let her go, knowing this was so wrong; anything he did to extend it would only make things worse.

Chynna was turning from him, slightly stunned. Her heart was beating in her ears like a drum. This was not what she'd expected. This was no shy man who needed coaxing at all. A sudden shot of fear spilled through her, and she pulled farther away, breathing hard, her eyes very wide, her hands flattened against his chest as though she needed a brace to protect her from him.

"That's enough for now," she said breathlessly, gathering the robe in close again. "I...I'd better go in."

He didn't try to stop her. Just as shocked as she was by what had happened, by that tiny, quick release that had sent them both spinning off their tracks, he sat back and didn't say a word, though inside he was swearing at himself. He stared after her as her white gown fluttered around her ankles. She disappeared into the house and slowly, very slowly, he lifted his face to the stars.

"I didn't mean to do that," he told them earnestly. "I really shouldn't have done that."

But they didn't give him any satisfaction at all. Shining down coldly, they seemed to mock him and his futile regrets. He swore again, aloud this time. What the hell had he been thinking? He wanted to get rid of her and instead, he'd damn near made love to her right out here on the grass.

Turning toward the woods, he made a gesture. "Were you watching that, Greg?" he asked the emptiness. "Did you see me kiss your bride-to-be?" Rising, he stared into the trees. "You'd better get home and take care of her, you jerk. If you don't, someone else will."

Someone else. Yeah, right. This was crazy, insane, and he had to get her out of here before something really happened. Groaning, he started off for the meadow. It would be too embarrassing to go in and take a cold shower at this point. A hard walk in the wild would have to do. And who knew? Maybe he'd find his brother out there.

Joe dreamed he was in Lilliput and a hundred little kids had him tied down on the beach, and when he woke up, he had the sense that someone was in the room with him. Blinking sleep out of his eyes, he looked around groggily. He'd left his door ajar, but now it was wide open.

"Who's there?" he called out accusingly.

There was a hush, and then a giggle, and then a flurry of moving bodies as Rusty sprang from behind the chair and headed for the door, and Kimmie leaped up from below the foot of the bed, running after him. And both children were shrieking at the top of their lungs, as though a demon were after them.

Joe groaned and pulled his pillow up over his head.

This was not the way he usually greeted the morning, and he had no intention of encouraging it, especially after the night he'd had. He'd spent an hour searching the woods for Greg after Chynna had gone in to bed. He'd looked everywhere, even at Greg's favorite camp-fire pit, but there was no sign of him. Then he'd come back to the house, rummaged through the kitchen until he'd found a half-empty bottle of Scotch, and he'd slugged it down, glass after glass, hoping to find some sort of answer in inebriation. Instead, he'd learned the age-old lesson: alcohol gives no insights; it only makes you dumber than ever.

He wondered, fleetingly, if Greg might have showed up during the night. But he knew this bedroom was the first place his brother would have come, and since he hadn't seen him, it was doubtful Greg had arrived.

Good. He wanted more sleep. He closed his eyes and tried to find it, but a few things got in the way. First, he felt as if his head were being used for practice by a very rough basketball team. Then there were the problems to be dealt with. But with this head, he was in no condition to think things through. No, he couldn't let the day intrude just yet. It was too early for him. He was on vacation, after all. He needed sleep, and slowly sleep began to creep over him again.

Then something horrible happened. The strains of a children's song began to filter in through his doorway. The kids had found the stereo and popped in one of their own tapes. He pulled the pillow down more tightly, but it didn't help. The childish voices just seemed to grow louder and louder. And sure enough, it was a song about whales. He gritted his teeth until it was over, then sighed with relief.

But his sense of deliverance didn't last long. They'd

found the Rewind switch. The song about the baby
whales came on again, loud and strong. He really
couldn't take this. Chynna's sexy voice crooning kids'
songs was one thing. A chorus of chipmunk voices
chirping about whales was something else. He had to
get rid of the hideous noise or go mad.

Blearily, he surveyed the situation. If he could get
the door closed, that might help. But he didn't want
to get out of bed. He thought for a moment, much as
it hurt his head to make the effort. If he threw his
extra pillow hard at the door, it might go back and hit
the wall and bounce out again, closing smartly. Yes,
that was the plan. Half sitting, he grasped the pillow
and heaved it, hard, at the door. As it sailed in the air,
seemingly going in slow motion, Chynna appeared in
the doorway, just in time to get smacked in the face
with the thing.

It was strange how slowly it happened. He watched
as the pillow seemed to hover in the air, watched as
she looked in and started to say something to him,
watched as the pillow hit and she staggered back.

And finally he sprang into action. Muttering a
stream of curses, he leaped out of bed and ran to her,
hitching up his baggy pajama bottoms as he went.

"Are you okay? God, I'm sorry, I really didn't
mean to do that. I wasn't aiming at you."

She stood there, bemused and slightly disheveled,
the pillow in her arms, and looked him up and down.
He was next to naked, and she decided right away she
liked what she saw. Hard, rounded muscles gave mute
testimony to the fact that the man worked out or
played a sport or something. A thatch of hair darkened
his chest and formed a trail below his navel, tantaliz-
ingly revealed by the raggedy, low-hanging pajamas.

"Then whom were you aiming at?" she asked, more interested than annoyed. "My kids?"

"I...no, I mean..." he stammered, shaken by the fear that her kids were exactly whom he would have liked to have thrown the pillow at. But you couldn't do things like that to kids. Could you? Dimly, he was pretty sure that was a no-no. "My door. I was trying..."

"Your door?" she repeated, glancing at the thing, then gazing at him askance. "I see."

He ran a hand through his tousled hair. It was much too early, and he was much too hungover to make sense of all this. "No, you don't see at all. I was aiming at the door so that it would hit the wall and then..."

She was shaking her head. "Greg, you don't have to explain. This is your house. You can throw pillows at people if you want to."

He started to say something defensive, then noted the sparkle in her eyes and realized she was teasing him.

He shook his head and gave her a quick grin, then held out his hand for his property. "Thanks for catching my pillow," he told her, pretending to be grumpy. "I'm going back to bed."

"Oh, no, you don't," she told him, hugging it to her chest. "It's late. You must be ready to get up by now. I feel like I've been waiting for you for hours."

Their eyes met, and the memory of the kiss from the night before flared up between them like a wall of fire. The kiss had told them both many things. It had told Joe he was attracted to his brother's bride, and it had told her he could be seduced by her. It had also told her she might find him a little harder to handle than she'd expected. But all in all, that wasn't bad. Still, it had been an experience neither of them would soon forget.

She looked away first, but he was the one who spoke.

"I didn't get much sleep last night," he explained, apologizing in his way. "I need to catch up. Another hour should do it."

Her head snapped up. "Another hour! It'll almost be time to go back to bed by then."

He gave her a flash of his crooked grin, even though it hurt his hair follicles to do it. "Great. Then I won't have to get up at all."

She rolled her eyes and glanced at the watch on her wrist. "Okay. We'll give you exactly one hour."

He held out his hand for his pillow again, but she ignored it. Coming on into his room, she made her way to the head of the bed, and put down the pillow herself, fluffing it up. But as she did so, her gaze fell on the empty Scotch bottle lying by the side of the bed, and her face changed. She glanced at his blood-shot eyes, looked back at the bottle and pressed her lips together.

"Just how much do you drink?" she asked, her voice tight, and he remembered that her ad in the catalog had specified no drinkers. Something told him that the man in her life—probably the father of these children—had been a drinker.

This was a lucky break, and he hadn't even planned for it. All he had to do was tell her he was a drunk, and she would be out of here like a shot. He could see it in her face. Just one little white lie and...

"I don't really drink at all." To his chagrin, he heard his own voice telling her the truth. "Last night was a special case. I had some things to think about and—" he shrugged "—I got carried away, and since I'm not used to drinking…"

She stared at him for a moment, searching his gaze, then seemed satisfied, though her eyes had a wary look she hadn't had before. She nodded slowly. "Okay."

He felt a sense of relief and could have kicked himself for it. What was the matter with him? He didn't want her to like him. That wasn't the point here. "Hey, don't forget," he told her quickly. "You're leaving today."

His announcement didn't seem to faze her. She glanced around the room and made a face. "You know, if you really don't want me for a wife, you might consider hiring me on as a surrogate mother," she said breezily, starting for the door. "From the condition this place is in, you need somebody."

Before he could answer, the tune struck up again and he winced, putting a hand to his throbbing head. Earplugs. That was what it was going to take. He rummaged through all the junk piled on Greg's dresser, but no earplugs appeared. Just as he was about to give up, he had a lucky break. There, on the floor, he spied a set of earmuffs left over from winter. Reaching down painfully, he pulled them out, and looked them over. They were very white and very fluffy, and he knew he was going to look like a fool if he put them on. But the baby whales were driving him crazy, and he tested them experimentally.

Chynna was still watching. "What are you doing?" she asked him curiously from the doorway.

He looked up and pulled one earmuff away from his ear. "What?"

"What are you doing?" she repeated.

"Defending myself from belugas," he admitted. The muffs were great for drowning out sound, but they were much too hot for this weather and would drive him nuts in their own way. He took them off and threw them back where he'd found them, then looked up at her again, annoyance plain on his face. "I'm thinking of joining a whaling expedition," he snapped. "Know where I can go to sign up?"

She stared at him for a moment, completely at sea, and then the words of the song sunk in and she smiled, realizing what the problem was.

"Don't think twice," she told him breezily. "I'll take care of it." She started toward the living room to stop the song in the stereo, but at the last second, she turned back. "How are you for songs about monkeys jumping on the bed?" she asked.

He made a face as he dropped to sit on the side of the bed. "Can't you find something soft and sultry? How about some Billie Holiday?" He rubbed his temples. "Now, there's a woman who understands these sorts of things."

"Hangovers?" She grinned as though she were doing so despite her better judgment. "I don't think the kids are ready for 'Lady Day,'" she told him as she disappeared from the doorway, closing his door as she went.

Probably not, he thought to himself as he lay back against the pillow and settled in. Children obsessed with baby belugas might not be ready to savor the intricacies of primal human tragedy.

"More's the pity," he muttered. "I'm feeling pretty damn tragic right now."

He put his head on the pillow and closed his eyes. The song had changed to monkeys, just as she'd promised, and she'd made them turn it down so that he could hardly hear it any longer. But still, he couldn't sleep. And it wasn't the music. Pictures of Chynna kept swirling through his mind, and as long as that was going on, he knew there was no part of his body that would let go.

It was nuts, this attraction he felt for her. Not only had she come to marry his brother, but she had two kids and a determined attitude that was the sort of thing that usually turned him off about a woman.

But when he came right down to it, he had to admit, over the years he'd developed a whole long list of things that turned him off about a woman. The older he got, it seemed the pickier he got. Deep down, he recognized the entire process was actually a way to guard himself against commitment. But that didn't bother him. Deep down, he didn't want to get married, so why not use every weapon he could against it?

Every now and then, he came up against a woman who shook his confidence in his bachelorhood. The last time it had been a painter he'd met on the beach at Malibu, an older woman who'd been as different as she was beautiful. She made pen-and-ink drawings of the passing scene, and he'd stopped by to comment. The next thing he'd known, they'd been involved in a deep philosophical discussion that had blown him away. She'd been a wiser, more original thinker than any professor he'd had in college. They'd gone for coffee, then for dinner, then for a weekend at Newport. She'd engaged his mind in the most-intellectual discussions he'd ever been a party to, and she'd shown him lovemaking like he'd never seen before. Only twenty-five, he'd fallen deeply in love, or he'd thought he had, anyway. He'd imagined their life together as a constant round of sex and contemplation, and he'd begun thinking marriage. Then her husband walked in to take her home, and Joe's plans, dreams and sense of being in love had fallen to ashes. That had taught him never to take anyone at face value. And he'd never let himself fall in love again.

"And never will," he told himself stoutly, and yet even he could tell there was a certain conviction missing at the moment. "That's a hangover for you," he murmured as he rose from the bed. Rationalization was the only way left to go, and sleep was going to continue to elude him, so he might as well get up and get this day over with.

Pulling on jeans and a polo shirt, and then his boots, he went out into the living room and headed for the kitchen, nodding at the children playing before the stereo as he passed them.

"Hi, kids," he grunted.

Kimmie's thumb went to her mouth as though it were magnetized, but Rusty managed an answer.

"Mornin', Mr. Camden," he said, watching wide-eyed.

Joe stopped and looked at him, appreciating the effort the kid had to make. "Call me Joe, okay?" he offered.

Rusty stared at him blankly, and he realized why as he made his way on into the kitchen and began to rifle through a cupboard. Rusty and Kim had followed him and were standing in the doorway. He glanced at them and saw they were still bewildered as he pulled down a box full of antacid tablets. They thought his name was Greg. Why would Greg ask to be called Joe? Poor kids. He glanced at them and hid a grin. Rusty definitely looked confused.

But this was no time for Joe to go into detailed explanations. His head was bouncing from one wall to the other, and he needed relief, fast. Grabbing a glass, he poured himself some water and dropped two tablets into it, watching as the liquid fizzed up, wincing as he thought of drinking the awful stuff.

"What's that?" Rusty asked, climbing up on a chair so that he could get a closer look.

Joe lifted the glass and looked at the bubbles. "This is a magic potion. It makes my head get smaller and my stomach stand still." Bracing himself, he gulped it down with his eyes closed, made a face and shuddered. He stood very still and waited for relief, and he got some pretty quickly. Looking down, he found both children staring at his head. For a moment, he was annoyed. Then he remembered what he'd told them. They were waiting to see it get smaller.

He hesitated, wondering how he could explain things to them, but nothing came to mind and he shrugged. Leaving the glass on the table and the box of tablets right next to it, he turned and left, heading for the bathroom. He needed to splash some water on his face and give himself a shave. Then maybe he would begin to feel human again.

Meanwhile, back in the kitchen, Rusty was reaching for the empty glass. Carrying it carefully, he set it on the counter near the sink, then began to edge the chair into position to give him access to water.

Kim watched him solemnly, then pulled her thumb out of her mouth, making a pop, like a cork from a bottle. "You gonna make your head small?" she demanded of her brother.

Rusty shook his head, busy with his chore. "Naw.

It didn't work. Didn't you see him? His head was the same size as ever."

Kim considered that for a long moment as Rusty turned on the faucet and filled the glass, then hopped down and got a handful of antacid tablets from the table, heading back toward the glass of water.

"But it's magic," she said at last.

Rusty nodded. "Yeah, I know. Look." He dropped two unwrapped tablets in the glass and they both watched it, openmouthed, as it did its fizzing routine.

"Wow," Rusty breathed.

Kim laughed and laughed, watching the bubbles with delight.

"Do more," she said when it began to calm down.

"Okay."

It was an easy reach from his position on the chair. He pulled down glass after glass, filled each and plopped in tablets, making a torrent of bubbles that made Kimmie laugh until tears ran down her cheeks. He didn't stop until he ran out of glasses.

"More," Kimmie cried. "Do more."

He shook his head sadly, looking at the three remaining tablets in his hand. "The glasses are all used up," he told her, looking bereft. Then an idea struck him, and his eyes brightened.

"Hey. Maybe goldfish like bubbles."

Kimmie nodded vigorously. "Yes, they do," she announced with all confidence. "Let's go."

And the two of them ran for the door, barely fitting through it as each pushed to be first.

Five

Chynna paused to listen to the call of a hawk. Pushing aside a curtain to look out the window, she was in time to catch its gliding flight into the woods. Now, why did that cry set up a feeling of happiness inside her, when the cry of the wolf the night before had filled her with fear?

"Daylight," she murmured to herself. "Everything seems less threatening in the day."

Of course, here in Alaska, there was more daylight at this time of year than anywhere else. "Which is why I'm going to love it here," she told herself resolutely.

She'd been cleaning up the den, putting things in stacks, working with a vengeance, and she hadn't yet admitted to herself she was doing all this to keep from thinking, to keep from facing facts. And now the cry of the hawk touched something inside her, and she knew it was time she made an inventory of her situation and decided what she was going to do next.

Flopping down into a big easy chair, she sighed and closed her eyes, letting her head drop back for a moment. For weeks, her mind had been filled with plans and the necessary detail work to cut all ties to Chicago and prepare for a new life in Alaska. She'd sold all her furniture, got rid of most of her clothes, shed boxes of children's toys and packed only the essentials for the trip north. A new, clean life, she'd thought. A haven for her children, a place where they could grow up knowing nature as an intimate ally rather than something they saw occasionally on the cable channels. A safe place, a place to grow and spread their wings, with limitless opportunities for their futures.

This was what she'd dreamed about since before Kimmie was born, since Kevin had died, since they'd been set adrift, like a little Family Robinson, on a sea of uncertainty, where the jobs were never good enough to pay for rent and day care, where every bill paid was another mountain scaled, where she was afraid to let her children out to play.

So she'd hit upon a plan. Why not get married again? She knew she would never love another man like she'd loved Kevin. But she could make a decent home for a man, in exchange for a decent home for her children. It seemed like a fair exchange. Why not?

She'd never taken it to the next step in her mind. She'd never let herself wonder what would happen if she arrived, kids and baggage in hand, and the man decided he didn't want her. She'd been so sure she could win him over. And yet...and yet...

She opened her eyes and stared out the window and the low, scudding clouds. Greg wasn't exactly falling head over heels for her, was he? He was a nice guy, attractive and likable. She'd really been lucky to have been chosen by him. The only problem was, he was having second thoughts. She had to get him past that, somehow.

Seduction. That might be the only way. And when she thought about the kiss they'd shared the night before, she knew it had possibilities. All she had to do was toughen herself up a bit. All she had to do was throw herself at the man. She grimaced. A fiercely independent person, she'd never begged for love before, and the thought of doing it now curdled her blood. But sometimes a woman just had to do what a woman had to do.

"You can do it," she whispered to herself encouragingly. "Flirt, darn you. It's the only way."

And as if to test out her resolve, Joe appeared in the doorway, looking a bit bleary, but otherwise as darkly handsome as ever.

"There you are," he said, as though he'd been looking for her. He glanced around the room and noted the change in the place, saw that she'd been cleaning.

"You really don't have to do this," he protested once again, but before he could go on, he noticed a copy of the catalog on top of a pile of papers she was throwing away.

"Oh, come on, you're not throwing out the catalog," he protested, picking it up and riffling through it. "I haven't finished looking at it."

She hated that catalog. It was a symbol of her desperate decision. She was happy with the results of that decision so far, but hated the thought that she'd had to stoop so low to get to this point.

"What do you need it for?" she said pertly, covering up the way she felt with a quick smile. "You've got me."

He looked up and into her eyes. "Greg has you. I'm not Greg."

Before she could react to that, his gaze fell on another pile of paper and magazines she'd made. "What is this?" he asked, frowning at what looked like a stack of old girlie magazines.

She looked down to see what he was referring to, then glanced up at his frown.

"Your reading material, I presume," she said, hiding a smile. "I'm trying to throw a lot of old things out and I'm making a pile of things I'm not sure about. You might want to look through it and let me know if you want to save any of them." She gestured toward the stack.

Joe looked from her down to the naked and very buxom woman on the cover. He stared at the picture for a moment too long, then quickly slapped another magazine on top of it, suddenly realizing, to his horror, that he was blushing beet red.

Chynna noticed and her eyes sparkled. "If these have been your girlfriends all these years," she said, teasing him with mock chagrin, "I don't know how you expect me to compete."

His mouth opened and then it closed again. He couldn't think of a thing to say. She'd thrown him off guard again, and he had to take a moment to get his coherence back. Funny how different she was from any woman he'd known before. There were times when he wasn't sure if she was laughing at him. Not that he minded. He was always ready for a good joke himself. Just as long as he was in on it. But these magazines were not his style, and he didn't want her to think they were.

Finally, he managed to defend himself. "These aren't mine. These are Greg's."

She winced and shook her head. "Greg, really, don't you think it's time to drop this charade?"

"No." He was getting annoyed himself, and when he slapped his hand down on the table to emphasize his point, the stack of magazines shifted, spilling out across the table and onto the floor, setting free a whole gallery of naked and half-naked ladies who laughed up at him. He hesitated, wanting to cover them, but short of throwing himself on top of them, there was no quick way to do it. Better to let it go, he realized. This was a case where he just couldn't win.

"No, because it's not a charade," he went on instead. "I don't know what I have to do to convince you I'm not Greg." He pulled out his wallet and flipped it open, wondering why he hadn't thought of this before. "Look at this. Joe Camden. I live in Los Angeles. See, here's my driver's license."

She stared at the document for a moment, nonplussed. What if he was telling the truth? She glanced at him. What if he really was not the man she'd come to marry?

Then who was Greg? And where was he?

No, she wanted this man to be Greg. She liked things just the way they were. There was only one adjustment needed. She had to make him want her.

"There's no picture," she noted, tapping her finger on the card.

He hesitated. "It's a renewal. I haven't had a ticket in years, so they just keep sending me these renewals. Here." He dug back into his wallet and pulled out the original, complete with murky picture. It had been in his back pocket so lóng, it had faded and was ragged around the edges. "There you go," he told her triumphantly. "That's me. See?"

She leaned close and scrutinized the picture. It looked to be a young man about fifteen years the junior of the man standing before her. The hair was lighter and worn long; the face was very different.

"That's not you," she said.

"What?" He looked at it, frowned and shook his head. He had to admit, it didn't look much like him now. "Sure, it's me. That was right after I graduated from college. Of course I looked different. But the basic guy is still the same."

He held it out, and she looked at it again, then smiled and patted his arm. "Nice try," she said dryly.

His tone mirrored his outrage at her obtuseness. "You don't believe a driver's license? An official document of the state government?"

She 'smiled at him. "Sure. I believe there is a Joe Camden. I just don't believe it's you."

"Listen." He swung to face her, his eyes shooting sparks as he tucked his wallet away again. "Let's look at this logically. If I'm Greg, I chose you out of a catalog, then sent you money to come join me. I would have been taking a gamble, sure, but you turned out pretty damn good. So why would I act like this? Why would I keep trying to send you away?" He shook his finger at her, obviously coming up with his trump card. "And why in God's name would I be keeping my hands off you?"

She shrugged, a bit taken aback by his vehemence. "I imagine you got cold feet about the whole thing, haven't you?"

He shook his head, exasperated with her. "What do you think I am, crazy? Or blind? A woman like you doesn't come along every day. If I were Greg, I'd have tested how things were between us by now. If I had a right to you..." He paused, aware that he was possibly saying things he shouldn't.

But she didn't want him to stop. A shiver of excitement sliced through her, and she moved closer, searching his eyes.

"What would you do?" she asked softly, touching his arm again. Her heart was beating hard in her throat, and she hoped he couldn't tell. Because this was it, the chance she'd been waiting for. If she didn't give things a little shove at this juncture, they might never get anywhere.

"What would I do?" he echoed numbly, his gaze riveted on her face. "That...that's not the point. The point is..." He hesitated. What the hell was the point? He couldn't remember. Her hand was moving on his arm, and his pulse was starting to throb.

"Chynna," he managed to murmur, reaching out to cover her hand with his and stop it from continuing to move on his flesh. "You'd better not..."

"What?" She still had another hand and she used it, placing it firmly against his chest and beginning a light massage. "Why don't we do it? Why don't we find out how things stand between us?"

A tempting thought, but one he had to ignore. He grabbed the hand on his chest, holding both still. "Because I'm not Greg," he told her gruffly.

She leaned toward him. "Then pretend you are," she whispered, lifting her face to make it simple for his lips to find hers.

He wasn't made of steel. Flesh and blood were all

he had, and neither was doing much to help him resist the temptation she placed before him. But he made one last attempt.

"No, Chynna," he muttered, shaking his head and trying not to notice how full and pink her lips were. "You don't belong to me. I can't pretend you do."

"I can," she said, slipping her arms from his and wrapping them around his neck, her body arching gently into him. "It's easy if you try."

The groan came from deep inside him. Her skin was smooth and cool, her mouth hot, her breasts soft and firm against his chest. He sank into her and felt as though he'd lost his balance, as though he were floating in a sea of sensation and only holding on to her would keep him from drowning.

She gasped softly as he took possession of her mouth. She'd had to coax him into doing this, but once started, the moves were all his, and she could feel his body respond, all hard muscle and hot desire. She hadn't been mistaken last night. He wanted her, wanted her badly, and this time his hands slid down her back and covered her bottom, drawing her hard up against him, as though he was determined to show her just what she was risking if she kept this up.

Sensation flooded her, scaring her with its intensity. She'd never responded to a man so rapidly, not even Kevin when they had both been so young and so deeply in love. What made her react to this man this way? She didn't know, and she wasn't sure she wanted to find out. Not yet, at any rate.

Gasping for breath, she pulled away from him, but this time it was much more difficult. He didn't let go easily, and as she slipped from him, he grabbed her hair and held her for a moment, looking into her face.

"Don't go starting things you're not prepared to finish, Chynna," he said huskily. "You can't turn me on and off like a switch."

"I...I'll finish this," she told him defensively, looking up into his smoky gaze and losing her breath again. "That's what I came for, after all. But not now, not with my kids in the next room. Tonight..."

He stared into her eyes, slowly shaking his head. "There won't be any tonight, Chynna." He let her go and turned away. "I told you you were going to have to go today," he reminded her. "And I meant it."

Her chin rose. She was shaky, but never a quitter. "And I told you, I'm not going."

Turning to look her over, he had to let a hint of a smile shade the light in his eyes. "What do you think you've got, squatters' rights on this old place or something?"

She caught the softening and gave it right back, smiling to take the sting out of her words. "I've got a contract, that's what I've got. Would you like to see it again?"

He groaned, shrugging his wide shoulders. "Don't you see that you can't stay here?" he demanded, then hesitated, knowing there had to be a better way to get to her, to get her to see this thing objectively.

"Listen," he said, striving for a reasonable tone, "you seem like such a modern, sort of feminist woman. If you lived here, you'd be quite isolated. How could you be happy staying home and raising kids? I mean, wouldn't you feel as though you'd been oppressed or something? It doesn't seem to be the thing to do any longer."

Chynna brightened. This was one of her favorite topics. She could be quite a crusader for traditional family values, and she was ready with her point of view. "Right," she said, letting a bit of sarcasm into her tone. "And while nobody's home raising the kids, you may have noticed that the world is pretty much going to pot in a lot of ways. Especially ways that have to do with turning good, healthy children into decent adults."

"I had heard some rumors to that effect." He gazed at her quizzically. He didn't know many women who would say a thing like that. But then, he didn't know many women like this one. "So tell me, what did you do before you began raising kids?"

"Career-wise?" She leaned back. "I worked for a large advertising agency. And believe me, while I was employed there, I lived for my job. And I did pretty well. But once I decided to have children, that became my job."

"And you've never regretted it?"

"Are you kidding? Landing a big account is nothing compared to watching your baby's eyes light up when he learns to read his first word or puts his puzzle together right for the first time. Those are the things that really count."

He had to admit, he still didn't get it. And he wasn't completely convinced. "So you're prepared to spend your whole life like this."

"What whole life? It's only a small chunk of my life. When they're fifteen or so, I'll probably start working again part-time, or start up my own business. And by the time they're off to college, I'll be ready to go back out into the world. And believe me, I'll still have a lot of life left in me." She smiled at him. "Life is a big cycle. A merry-go-round. You can jump on and off when you feel like it."

She certainly had herself convinced. He shook his head. "Well, you see, that's another reason why you shouldn't stay. You'll never be able to get a job out here. Or even start your own business."

She didn't know when to admit defeat. Her chin rose, and she pinned him with a direct gaze. "Why not? I noticed someone had a nail parlor in town. I could do something like that."

"In town?" He snorted derisively. "You come from Chicago and you can call that bump in the road a town?"

He couldn't shake her enthusiasm for the place. "It's as much town as we'll need."

He shook his head, beginning to think there was no getting through to her. "But, Chynna, you've got to face it. You're not staying."

"Why not?" she asked, ready to fight for her future and that of her children if she had to.

He threw his arms out as though he could encompass the whole kit and caboodle. "You just can't. Can't you tell? Look how primitive it is here."

"I can take primitive," she said stubbornly. "I'll camp out if I have to. I signed a contract to marry Greg Camden."

He shook his head slowly, impressed despite how much she annoyed him. "And you're going to stick to that contract come hell or high water. Is that it?"

She met his gaze with head held high. "Damn right."

He stared at her for a long moment. That made it even worse. She was promised to Greg and she meant to stay that way. Joe had no right to touch her and he quickly vowed it would never happen again. Turning, he began to make his way out of the room.

"Where are you going?" she asked, as though she was afraid he would head for the hills just as he claimed the real Greg had done.

"I'm going out to take a look at what condition the barn and stables are in," he told her without looking back.

"What should I do with these magazines?" she called after him.

He slowed, then turned back and looked her full in the face. "Burn them. Throw them away. What the hell? I don't need them. If I want to look at a sexy woman, all I have to do is look at you."

"Well, thank you, kind sir," she murmured, flushing just a bit, but he was long gone and she was talking to herself. Still, it was reassuring. Somehow she was going to turn him around.

She packed up her cleaning things and headed for the kitchen, humming a tune under her breath. She'd expected to see the children in the living room with the stereo, but she didn't worry when they weren't there. She was sure they were playing quietly someplace about. She was still humming when she stepped into the kitchen, but the hum stuck in her throat when she saw the mess that awaited her. Glasses stood everywhere, some still full of liquid, some on their sides with the liquid spilling out onto the floor. The empty antacid wrappers gave mute testimony to what had been going on, and when she heard Kimmie giggling in the front room, she spun and headed for the sound.

"Look at Goldie!" she heard Rusty saying. "He likes it. He really likes it."

And with dread in her heart, she ran into the room.

The barn was a mess. It hadn't been used in years. But the stables were okay. Greg seemed to have a horse, probably the animal he was on right now as he rode his way through the mountains, avoiding the bride he'd thought he wanted to marry.

Joe could remember when the stables had been full and the barn the best stocked in the valley. His father had been an unusual man, but he'd worked hard and run his piece of land like a ship at times. At others, he would disappear into the wilderness and not come home for weeks. The family had stayed on for a few years after he'd died, but things had gone downhill. His mother had done the best she could, but she'd never loved the place the way his father had. She'd spent most of her last few years there concentrating on preparing Joe for college, and then for law school. Meanwhile, Greg had headed for the hills every chance he got, playing at being mountain man. There was no one to take care of the land the way it needed, and Joe had settled in L.A., and their mother had moved to Anchorage, but Greg had stubbornly held on, not wanting any part of anything but the Alaskan wild.

"He's wasting his life out there," their mother had said time and time again. "If only he would get some education and make something of himself."

Joe had been impatient with him, too, but that hardly made a dent in Greg's enjoyment of life. In fact, the more angry he made Joe, it often seemed, the happier he was himself. If Greg had known his brother was coming to see him, Joe could almost see him setting up this situation with Chynna just to torture him. But he couldn't have known. Could he?

As he was pondering this mystery, he heard a new sound and it echoed in his memories before he placed it. Someone was arriving on horseback. Turning, he saw the man coming in through the gate. His hair was long, his beard full, his clothes old-fashioned and worn. His saddle was hand tooled, and an old Indian blanket lay under it.

For just a moment, he wondered if it might be Greg. But no, this man was older. He was the picture of a mountain man, though, the sort of man who'd haunted the mountains of the West for over two hundred years. From the evidence he saw before him, he would wager this man hadn't been anywhere within smelling distance of real civilization for decades. Or anywhere near a shower in quite some time, either.

The man reined in his horse and looked down at Joe.

"Howdy," he said. "Heard you got a woman needs taking care of."

Joe's head went back, and his eyes narrowed. "You heard what?"

The man shifted his weight and looked toward the mountains. "Heard you got a woman who came to marry your brother and he lit out."

Joe shook his head, amazed at the way news traveled. "Where did you hear about that?"

The man looked down at him and shrugged. "I was out drinking with some of the boys last night, and it came up."

"Wonderful," Joe said with all the sarcasm he could muster. "So we're the item of the week, are we?"

The man looked slightly puzzled. "I don't rightly know about that," he declared, quieting his restless horse with a touch of his hand on the neck.

Joe sighed, feeling beleaguered. "No, I suppose

not,'' he muttered. He'd come on a simple errand. All he'd wanted to do was grab Greg and take him to Anchorage to see his mother. Instead, he was facing new complications at every turn. And people said living in L.A. was stressful. He looked up at the man, who was speaking again.

"Anyway, thought I'd come on down and see if I could help you out," he said, his shifty gaze flitting from one side of the yard to another, then settling on the house, as though he was looking for evidence that the woman might be nearby.

Joe put a hand up to shade his eyes from the sun. "Oh, yeah?" he said, and he could hardly keep the belligerence he felt from his tone. After all, this man could couch it in these polite terms, but what he really wanted was to take Joe's woman away from him. At least, that was the way it looked to Joe. "And what had you planned to do to help me out?" he asked, amused that the man thought he had a chance.

The man leaned forward in the saddle, as though he was going to confide in Joe. "I just wanted to let you know, if she's pretty, I reckon I could marry her myself."

Joe held back his grin, but it wasn't an easy thing to do. "And if she's not so pretty?"

He shrugged and got honest. "She'd have to be ugly as a badger not to look pretty to me. I been alone so long, I pretty much forgot what a woman was until this thing came up about you having an extra one."

An extra one. It might be amusing to see what Chynna would think of that. But he really didn't want to get Chynna involved here. Much as the man might divert him, there was an underlying sense of menace he couldn't deny. Joe stared into the man's fiery eyes and noted his long, greasy beard and then his gaze dropped to the thirty-aught-six rifle he held in his callused hands.

"Well, she's pretty, all right," he told him. "But I'm afraid she's just not your type. She's real squeamish—you know what I mean? She hates dirt and she hates the wind and she hates the wolves. She pretty much hates Alaska at this point, and she can hardly wait to get out of here. In fact, I'm trying to find a way to get her back to Anchorage." He shook his head sadly. "Afraid you missed the boat on this one. She won't be here long enough to court and all."

The mountain man shifted the chaw of tobacco he was chewing from one side to the other. "Hey, a week might be long enough for me," he muttered. "Let's have a look at her."

Joe glanced at the rifle again. "If you want a woman that badly, why not go on into Anchorage one of these days and find yourself some likely little gal who would come out here and do for you?"

The man gave him a look as though he'd suggested they try taking cooking classes together. "I can't go near that place."

Joe shrugged. "Well, I'm sorry I can't help you."

"No," the man said, leaning down and staring at Joe, "I'm sorry *I* can't help *you*."

"Oh. Right." He tried a pleasant smile. "Well, so long."

The man turned his horse, and then Joe remembered something.

"Do you know my brother, Greg?" he called after him.

The man twisted in the saddle. "Yup," he said.

"You seen him anywhere?"

"Nope."

Joe grimaced. "Well, if you see him, tell him I'm looking for him, would you?"

The man hesitated. "I seen someone who's seen him," he offered.

Joe's hope perked up again. "Where?"

"Said he was up on yonder mountain. Said he was hunting."

"Oh. I guess he'll be back when he's back."

"More 'n likely. So long."

"So long."

Joe watched him go and debated telling Chynna about him. In the end, he decided to hold back the story at this time. But he knew even more firmly that he had to get her out of here and on her way back home. An unattached woman in a male bastion like this was bound to cause problems. He wasn't about to spend his days fighting off men who wanted to carry her off to live in their caves with them. He had enough problems fighting himself off her.

He made his way back to the house. Chynna met him at the door, and her pretty face was a mask of tragedy.

"Greg, I'm really, really sorry. I hope...well, I don't know for sure, but we may be able to save one of them."

"What?" A genuine sense of alarm flashed through him. What had happened? Was something wrong with the kids? "What are you saying?"

She hesitated, looking the very picture of regret. "Your goldfish. Goldie and Piranha."

He stared at her blankly, then realized what she was talking about. "Ah, yes, the goldfish. What about them?"

She bit her lip, her dark eyes troubled. She was well aware that he hadn't warmed to her children. This would be another black mark against them, no doubt. But she wouldn't hide it from him. The best way to deal with it was to be up front about it and take the lumps that came her way. Anything else would just poison things in the future.

"Well," she began, "the kids saw you using antacid this morning..."

"And?"

"And they dropped a couple of the tablets in the goldfish bowl," she added in a rush.

He frowned. "They what?"

"I'm sorry." She shook her head. "And so are they. Kimmie's crying now that she realizes it might kill the goldfish. I've got them in fresh water, and they're floating, but they still seem to be breathing, and..."

"Chynna..." He was laughing. She stared at him, appalled and outraged, but he couldn't stop. "I thought you were talking about your children at first," he told her between chuckles. "And then I realize it's only goldfish. Believe me, I'll survive the loss, should the worst come to pass."

"Well, I may not," she said in a harried tone, her hair looking a little wild, her eyes looking a little wilder. She was relieved that he hadn't reacted with annoyance, but she'd been through an emotional roller-coaster ride in the past hour and she was going to take time to recuperate. "Rusty's already planning a funeral service. He wants me to make a eulogy."

Joe grinned. "No problem. Goldfish eulogies are easy."

"Oh, yeah?" She let her shoulders sag. "Then why don't you do it?"

"Oh, no," he said, looking very wise. "It would be better coming from you. After all, you're the caring, compassionate sort of person. I'm the cold, heartless realist." He laughed softly, finding this entire situation vastly amusing. "And anyway, you spawned these little goldfish murderers. It's your responsibility."

Finally, she relaxed. It looked as though it wasn't going to be quite the crisis she was afraid of when she first found her two kids with the poor fish gasping for oxygen.

"They're good kids," she told him with a quick smile. "I hope you're considering leniency."

His smile faded, and he turned away. There was no point in beating around the bush. Things had to be faced.

"Actually, I'm considering banishment for all three of you," he said, trying to keep his tone light but not really succeeding. "Get your kids together. We're going into town. I'm going to get you transportation back to Anchorage if I have to hire sled dogs to take you."

Six

"It's going to be a long drive to Anchorage. I'll drop you off at the store so you can stock up with some snacks and things for the kids."

Chynna looked at her children in the back seat and then turned her attention to Joe. "Where are you going while we're in the store?" she asked him quietly.

He glanced at her. "I'm going to find someone to drive you back," he said shortly, then stared straight ahead as though he didn't trust himself to go into it any further.

Chynna stared ahead, as well, but she didn't see the landscape, or even the snow-covered mountain peaks in the distance. Her stubborn streak was rising in her chest. He could make all the arrangements he wanted to make, but what he did had no bearing on what she did. After all, if he wasn't willing to honor their contract, he had no claim on her. And there was no way she was leaving.

The little collection of shacks that masqueraded as a town came into view, and she leaned forward, eager to see it again. It reminded her of the set of a Western movie, with boardwalks and false fronts, and a severe lack of recent paint jobs. But there was something endearing about it, and she'd warmed to it, right from the beginning.

"Ask for Annie," he told her as he dropped her off in front of the general store. "She'll set you up with everything you need."

"What I need is a husband," she murmured to him with a significant look before turning to help her children get out of the car.

"Just ask Annie," he said, trying to maintain a light tone. "She's liable to have a supply of them, too."

Her look had daggers, and she tossed her head as she turned from him and started up the steps with her children. He drove off slowly, looking back in his rearview mirror, but she pretended not to notice.

She paused in the doorway, looking in. The place had an atmosphere that conjured up pictures of stores at the turn of the century, and in truth, had probably been established sometime around that age. A group of men sat around the stove, although the weather was too warm to need to have it lit, most of them on chairs tilted back, leaning against the wall. The room itself was well stocked with canned and packaged goods stacked on shelves that filled the walls, all the way to the ceiling.

The men were talking lazily, but as she entered, tilted-back chairs came back to rest on all fours with a thud, and a hush fell over the group. They each gaped at her and her children as though they'd never seen anything like them.

The reception was rather disconcerting, but she smiled and asked, "Does anyone know where I can find Annie?"

There was a pause, and then they all tried to talk at once. At the same time, a gray-haired woman with lively dark eyes came out of a back room and stood behind the counter.

"May I help you?" she asked, looking Chynna over with an alert intelligence Chynna responded to immediately.

Chynna came forward and gave Annie her name and introduced the children. "We flew in yesterday on the mail plane," she began.

Annie didn't let her get any further. Her jaw dropped and her eyes snapped. "Don't tell me you're the one who came to be Greg's wife," she exclaimed.

Chynna hesitated. "Well, yes, I did."

"Oh, darling..." Annie grabbed her hand and pumped it up and down. "Well, what do you know. Greg hinted there was someone coming to join him, but I never dreamed you'd be so...you'd be..."

"So darn pretty," piped up one of the men who had been sitting around the stove. He'd risen and was coming over to join them at the counter. "Greg is a lucky man."

Chynna turned, flushing, and found that her children had gathered around another man who was pulling quarters out of the air much to the delight of the little ones. That was reassuring. She didn't want to talk about Greg in front of the kids, and now that they were occupied, she wouldn't have to be quite so circumspect. She turned back to Annie.

There was something in the woman's face that inspired confidence and brought up the urge to unburden herself. And she sure needed someone to confide in. Annie looked ready to hear her out, and the man who'd come up to lean on the counter—Annie called him Roger—had a face full of sympathy. These were people she'd never seen before, but somehow that made it even easier to tell them the truth.

"Well, the problem is," she said softly, "it doesn't look like Greg wants me after all."

Annie's face registered shock. "Doesn't want you?" She slapped her hand down on the counter. "That sniveling little polecat. How dare he not want you?"

Chynna was a little startled by this description of the handsome man she'd been with for the past twenty-four hours. But Roger muttered his agreement with the sentiment.

"He's a fool—that's what he is. Always was a fool. Saw him keep a skunk for a pet once. Knew he was a fool ever since."

Chynna couldn't imagine the man she knew keeping skunks, but she supposed she didn't really know him very well. "At any rate, he wants us to go back to Chicago as soon as possible."

Annie shook her head. "Well, we heard there was some problem, but I was sure it would blow over as soon as Greg got his courage up."

"He should cut that wild long hair of his," Roger said, shaking his head. "Maybe then he'd be able to hear the advice everyone keeps giving him."

"Hair?" Chynna frowned. Greg didn't have long hair. He certainly must have had a haircut since the man had seen him last.

"Yeah, 'Grizzly Greg' we call him around here,"
Roger went on. He smiled at Chynna, looking a bit
sheepish. "When he first told us fellas he was sending
away for a bride, we all thought he was loco. But
seeing you, I guess there are more men who will want
to take a look at that book he found you in."

Annie was impatient with this line of talk. She
wanted to stick to the main point. "You say Greg
wants you to go back where you came from." She
looked at Chynna sharply. "He said this to your
face?"

She nodded. "He's made it very clear. He's out
looking for a way to send us back to Anchorage to
catch a plane for home right now."

Annie pursed her lips. "Listen. We don't have
many women out here in Dunmovin. And the ones we
got...well, we've got to stick together." Reaching out,
she patted Chynna's hand. "You come on into the
back room with me. I'll fix you a nice cup of tea and
we'll talk."

"But my kids..."

"Don't you worry about them. We'll take care of
them. Henry!" She gestured toward the man who'd
just found a dime in Rusty's ear, much to the boy's
amazement. "Take those kids out back and show them
Cleo and her babies. They'll like that." She nodded
at Chynna. "Cleo's a fat old sow but she does have
the cutest little piglets."

Chynna began to shake her head, sure that her children, who'd been through a lot in the past two days,
would want to stick close to her rather than go off
with a stranger. But as she turned, she saw the old-
timer reach out to Rusty and Kim with both hands,
and to her amazement, she saw those same children

reach right back, and in no time their pudgy little fingers were being held tightly and they were being led out back. And neither one of them so much as looked back over a shoulder to see what Mom was doing.

"Oh, Henry's a wonder with the kids," Annie told her, reading the surprise in her face. "They'll be fine. You come on with me."

She did just that, following her through a doorway and settling down with a sigh as the older woman ran water for tea. The room was nicely furnished and looked nothing like the store area looked. She sat in a comfortably upholstered chair and examined the pictures on the wall.

"Your children?" she guessed, gesturing at the pictures of young soldiers and an airplane.

"Yup, those are my boys. Jack and James. They both went into the service and neither one of them ever came back."

"Oh, I'm so sorry," Chynna began, but Annie laughed.

"No, honey, I don't mean they died. They both ended up living in California. Both married. And I hardly ever get to see my grandchildren."

She poured out the hot water and stood back, smiling at the younger woman. "Oh, they invite me to come on down there and live with them often enough. But I tell them I've got Alaska in my blood. I can't leave her."

Chynna smiled. "It certainly is beautiful here," she said. "The scenery is so dramatic."

Annie nodded, pouring out the tea into two cups. "You should see it in the winter. It's like another world."

Chynna sighed. "I'm not sure I'll get to see that,"

she said. "Unless I find a way to avoid it, it looks like I might be leaving very soon."

Annie frowned, studying her face with a cool, perceptive look. "You don't want to go? You'd like to stay?"

Chynna hesitated, then nodded. "I don't want to go back. I think this place would be perfect for raising my kids."

"Your kids." Annie nodded slowly, as though she understood fully. "They're why you came in the first place, aren't they?"

Chynna nodded. "Not that I would have short-changed Greg in any way," she added hastily. "I was prepared to be a good wife. But my main motivation was to find a place where I could raise my children."

Annie made a sound of disgust. "That darn Greg," she muttered, throwing down her napkin.

Chynna shook her head, anxious not to be misunderstood. "Don't blame Greg," she told her quickly. "It's really my own fault. You see, I tricked him. I..." Funny how easy it had been to do this and how hard it was to explain it to people. "I didn't tell him about Rusty and Kimmie."

She stared. "He didn't expect the children?"

Chynna nodded. "I gambled that he'd learn to love them so quickly, it wouldn't make any difference. But I lost that gamble. And now I realize it was unfair of me to spring it on him this way. I'm only getting what I deserve. I just wish..."

"Well, I can see that the kids came as a shock to him. I'm sure he had fantasies of things children tend to inhibit." Annie looked at her fiercely. "Are you in love with the guy?"

She hesitated. "Well, I hardly know him. But..."

She looked at Annie's skeptical face. She would have been skeptical, too, only hours before. But now... "Why? Does that seem so impossible to you?"

Annie shrugged and looked a little uncomfortable. "To tell you the truth, I can't remember any other girl loving Greg. I wouldn't have thought it could happen that fast. I would have thought he would be more of an acquired taste."

"I like him very much," Chynna said, realizing that what she'd just said was an understatement. "He seems like a really quality person."

Annie grimaced. "Greg?" she asked softly.

But Chynna didn't notice. She was thinking very hard, remembering his gentleness with the children, even though he obviously didn't understand them, how embarrassed he'd been about the girlie magazines, how he'd resisted her when she'd tried to coax him with sexual attraction—even though his resistance hadn't lasted very long. And then she thought of his kiss and how she had reacted, heart and soul, and a sadness filled her. She'd never thought another man could take Kevin's place. Even though he'd been dead for three years, she'd never been tempted to fall for anyone else. Until now. And she had to admit, she was tempted. Too bad he felt so very differently.

"Well, what does Joe say about all this?" Annie was asking.

"Joe?" Chynna's head rose in surprise, and after a heartbeat, a feeling of gathering doom began to settle in her heart. "You mean Greg's brother?"

Annie nodded and grinned as she thought of him. "He was in here yesterday. It was sure good to see him. He's been living down in Los Angeles for years. But I guess you know that."

A strange buzzing had set up shop in Chynna's ears. She took a long sip of tea and said, her voice forced, "They...they're not much alike, are they?"

"Oh, no," Annie said, laughing and motioning dismissively with her free hand. "Tell you the truth, Greg has always been a bit of a pain in the neck. But Joe..." She smiled. "Joe's a sweetheart. I've always had a soft spot for that boy. He's almost like a third son to me."

Annie went on, filling in anecdotes from years past, and though Chynna laughed and nodded, she wasn't listening. She was numb. He'd been telling the truth all along. Joe wasn't Greg. *Oh my.*

Finally, she had to laugh. Annie had just told about how Joe had sent away for a superhero uniform and worn it everywhere he went when he was eight, so the laughter seemed appropriate to her. But the more Chynna laughed, the more she realized that it had nothing to do with Annie's stories, but her own amusement and horror at the mistakes she'd made.

When she finally ran out of laughter, she turned very serious very quickly.

"Listen, Annie," she said leaning forward and fixing the woman with a direct gaze. "We don't know each other well, but I need advice. Do you think you can help me?"

Annie blinked and nodded slowly. "I took a liking to you from the moment I saw you," she told Chynna. "And I'm seldom wrong about people. Go ahead and ask, honey. I'll do anything I can to help you."

Chynna smiled and took the woman's hand in hers. "Thank you," she said, her eyes full of sincere appreciation. "Now, here's what I need."

* * *

Chynna and the kids were watching for Joe and they came out as he drove up in front of the store. Annie came out with them, chatting with Chynna and herding the kids in to the back seat of the car while Chynna stowed the bags of groceries away. Finally, Annie bent down and spoke to Joe.

"You take good care of this girl. And tell Greg I'm going to give him what for the next time I see him. Imagine, not wanting a girl like this, and after she's come all that way, too!"

Joe swung around in surprise and met Chynna's gaze. She smiled at him, looking just a bit sheepish, and murmured, "Please don't say I told you so."

He grinned, relieved and regretful all at the same time. "Not even once?"

"No. You say it, and I'll find some way to make you pay."

He chuckled. It was about time. There had been advantages to being thought of as Greg, he had to admit, but all in all, he preferred his own identity. And he was glad Chynna wasn't going to leave thinking this was all his fault.

They all waved at Annie as the car started down the road toward home. Glancing into the back seat, Joe's gaze met Rusty's, and he noted that the boy was fairly jumping up and down in his seat, his eyes alight, his face full of excitement.

"Hey, what's got you so stoked?" he asked the child.

Rusty didn't need any more of an invitation to tell him. "We had fun," he told him, his dark eyes huge. "We saw baby pigs. They were little and they squealed, just like this." He gave a tiny sound that had both Joe and Chynna laughing, then went on.

"And the man—he pulled a dime out of my ear. Just like this." He demonstrated. "Mom, could I learn to do tricks like that? Could I learn magic?"

"I don't know," Chynna said, tousling his hair. "Magic takes a lot of work. You'd have to practice very hard."

"Maybe the man could teach me," Rusty said.

"Maybe. We'll have to ask him next time we see him."

Joe looked up quickly, catching her glance. He'd noted the reference to a future in this area, and that didn't fit with the facts as he knew them. But she merely smiled at him, looking like the cat that ate the canary, and he felt he had to put in his two cents' worth.

"There are probably places you can take magic classes back in Chicago," he told Rusty, glancing over his shoulder at the boy. "Maybe your mother will look into them when you get back."

"But...but Mom says we're going to live here now," Rusty said, and then he seemed to remember that he wasn't supposed to be friends with Joe, that he'd made some secret and private pact against it, and he lapsed back into silence in his corner of the car. Kimmie spent the whole time with her thumb in her mouth, staring at the back of Joe's head, but not making a sound.

Chynna looked back at them both, smiled and winked and didn't say another word. Joe was silent the rest of the way back, as well, but he wasn't very cheerful. There seemed to be too much to think about for that.

First off, there was Chynna. She was acting far too happy. He knew she didn't want to leave, knew she

had been upset to think he was making concrete plans
to get transportation for her and her children. He'd felt
guilty earlier, knowing how much it must have cost
her to come, emotionally, mentally, and in giving up
all that she'd left behind. He knew her well enough
by now to know she would feel she had failed if she
left. But she had to leave. He had to get her out of
here before Greg showed up. The better he knew her,
the more sure he was that she would be crazy to marry
his brother.

At the house, the children tumbled out of the car as
soon as their seat belts were released and they ran
across the yard to swing on a loose gate, and Chynna
leaned on the porch railing, watching them with a bittersweet smile. This was exactly what she wanted for
them, a place where they could run and play and ex-
plore life without worrying about a kidnapper or a bus
coming down on top of them. She wanted them to
watch ants build a hill and find quail eggs in the
bushes and see a sunrise reflected on the nearby lake.
This was what she'd bargained for. And though she'd
lost at her first try, she had another trick up her sleeve.
The only question was, did she have the guts to go
through with it?

Joe came up behind her and watched the children
playing, as well. Turning, she smiled at him. "I'm
sorry," she said softly.

He gazed down into her velvet brown eyes and felt
something stir deep inside. "There's nothing for you
to be sorry about," he said gruffly, avoiding the emotion that threatened to rise in him, pushing it back
where it belonged.

She nodded. "Yes, there is. I refused to believe you

when you were telling me the truth. I guess I just wanted you to be Greg so badly...."

"Never mind," he said quickly. "That's all over now."

"I came thinking I would be getting married. I guess that's all over, too." She gave him a teasing, melancholy smile. "I don't suppose *you'd* like to get married?"

He shook his head. Though he knew if ever there was a woman he might consider it with... But no, marriage was not for him. And children were something he didn't understand and didn't want to know more about. "I don't think I'm the marrying kind," he told her.

She nodded sadly. "I was afraid of that."

It was his turn to give her a slow grin. "But thanks for asking."

Her chin rose, and she turned back to watch the children. "Don't get too swellheaded over it," she advised him dryly. "I would have asked any good-lookin' man."

He grinned, recognizing a face-saving put-down when he heard one. "If it's just anyone you want, you won't have to wait long. I've had three men ask about you today. One of them rode right into the yard, ready to take you back to his cabin or whatever he lives in."

She turned as though delighted with the news. "Why didn't you tell me? I could have looked them over. Had my pick."

He gave her a look that said he still thought she was nuts and then he slumped down to sit on the top step. "Tell you what," he said, looking up at her with a grin. "If another guy shows up, I'll bring him right on in to meet you, and you can tell him to his face whether he makes the grade or not.''

Dropping down to sit on the step below his, she gazed up at him with pretended skepticism. ''Something tells me you wouldn't be laughing if this were really a good idea.''

He chuckled. ''Don't be so cynical. We've got some great men out here in Dunmovin. The fact that most of them haven't shaved in ten years and probably haven't had a bath since Christmas—that's all superficial stuff. You can turn a man like that around on a dime—I have no doubt.'' He shook his head, his eyes dancing. ''It's almost a shame that you won't have your chance with Greg. It would have been interesting to see what you would have done with him.''

Interesting, was it? That was a word that usually meant trouble in her experience. She drew her legs up and wrapped her arms around her knees. ''So Greg really is up in the mountains hiding away someplace,'' she said softly, and she couldn't resist glancing toward the trees.

Joe picked up a pine needle and began to pull it apart. ''Yup. He really is.''

She didn't turn to look at him. ''Why is he hiding?''

Joe was silent for so long, she almost turned to look at his face, to try to gauge what he was thinking. But he finally spoke. ''I figure he ordered you in a drunken stupor and then liked the idea of you. But when you told him you were really coming, he couldn't quite face the reality of you. So he took off, figuring you'd leave when you couldn't find him.''

She looked toward the woods again, almost imagining she could see movement in the shadows. ''Are you saying he's out there right now, watching us?'' she asked him softly.

He shrugged. ''Could be. I wouldn't put it past him.''

She was quiet for a few minutes, and then softly, very softly, she began to sing a song about a bird in a cage, and about its mate left alone in the forest, about how they both died of broken hearts.

Leaning back against the post, he half closed his eyes and let the sound wash over him. There was something about her voice that took the starch out of his muscles and made him feel about to melt all over, and that was unusual for him. He prided himself on toughness—in life and in the courtroom, but when he heard her sing…wasn't there some legend about a woman who could weave a spell with her voice, disarm an army? That was what Chynna's singing did to him.

Her song was over and she looked at him, smiling, and for just a moment, he thought she was going to lean over him and touch his face—maybe kiss him. The look was in her eyes. And his heart began to beat a little faster, anticipating.

But she merely patted his jeans-clad knee and drew back again. ''If you won't marry me, maybe you ought to hire me,'' she said lightly. ''It looks like I could put you to sleep anytime, anywhere.'' Rising, she laughed down at him, then turned and went into the house.

Joe sat back up and blinked, trying to analyze the way she could manipulate his blood pressure. He'd never felt so vulnerable to an outside influence before, and it sort of scared him. ''Oh, well,'' he told himself.

"She'll be out of my life soon. Then I won't have to worry about it."

She'd gone off before he'd had a chance to tell her about the arrangements he'd made for her trip. But that was okay. He didn't want to talk about them. He wasn't going to relish seeing her go. But he would be relieved to know she was on her way back to Chicago and out of Greg's sphere of influence.

She fixed the kids a late-afternoon snack, chattering with them, and including him when he came and sat at the table, drawn by the happy sounds. The children were subdued when he joined them, but Rusty soon loosened up and by the end of the meal, was almost natural. Kimmie, however, never took her thumb out of her mouth and never took her wary gaze off Joe.

"I'm starting to worry about her," Chynna admitted to him when Rusty had run off to play. Kimmie sat before her plate where not a thing had been touched. "I don't think she's eaten anything since we got here yesterday."

Joe frowned. Feeding kids was something he didn't know much about, but he didn't like to think of anyone going hungry on his account. "Has she had anything to drink?" he asked, just to make sure it wasn't time to call the doctor.

"Yes, she's had a little juice. And one glass of milk that I know of."

"Then she's probably okay," he said reassuringly, though they both knew he didn't have a clue as to what it all meant. He moved closer to the little girl and smiled at her. "Don't you want to have a bite of this sandwich?" he asked her, indicating the food on her plate. "It looks very yummy to me."

Kimmie leaned as far away from him as she could

get without falling out of the chair. Her blue eyes were wide and vigilant. It was pretty obvious there was no way she was going to eat anything on Joe's say-so.

He stared at her, at the look in her eyes, at the lack of trust, and suddenly, he wanted more than anything in the world to make this little girl like him. It was something he had to do. He sat beside her and studied the situation. She wouldn't eat. She wouldn't speak. She wouldn't let him touch her. What could he do to get through to her?

Little girls liked dolls, but he didn't have any of those. They had tea parties, but he was afraid he didn't have tiny teacups in his old trunk in the bedroom. What else did they like? Animals?

Animals. Hmm.

"Hey, Mr. Camden, want to come watch me climb a tree?" Rusty was in the doorway, hesitating, looking hopeful, but ready to withdraw the invitation if he got the slightest indication it was unwelcome.

"Mr. Camden doesn't have time to..." Chynna began, but Joe rose and grinned at the boy.

"Sure, I'll come watch," he told him. "I used to climb that old elm outside my bedroom window when I came home late at night and my brother locked me out."

"Really?" Rusty was impressed. "Did you ever fall?"

"A hundred times."

"Yeah." Rusty looked relieved. "Sometimes you just gotta fall, huh?"

"Sometimes you do."

Joe threw Chynna a smile as he followed the boy out, and Chynna held her breath, holding back her heartbeat. The man was so...so... What could she say?

Another man might have brushed Rusty off. Another man might have had to say he never fell, might have had to prove how manly and powerful he was, just to put the kid in awe. But not Joe. He saw immediately what the boy needed, and he gave it to him. For just a moment, her eyes filled with tears.

"Thank you, Mr. Camden," she said softly, and then she looked down to see Kimmie looking up at her, so silent, so watchful, and she bent down to kiss the top of her head. "And thank you, Miss Kimmie, for being my good girl. Now, how about eating just one bite? Look—this sandwich sure looks like a tiny airplane to me. Here it goes, taking off at the airport. And it's flying around and around." Swooping the sandwich through the air, she made the appropriate airplane sounds. "It's ready to land! Better open up the hangar! It's coming in." She slowly swooped the sandwich toward Kimmie's face, but the hand didn't move. The thumb still plugged the entryway. "Open up! Quickly!"

Kimmie's eyes looked very sad, but she resolutely shook her head. She was not going to eat. Not tonight.

"Oh, Kimmie." She dropped the sandwich down on the plate. "Look. The airplane had to crash. It couldn't get into the hangar."

She looked at Kimmie again, but the wall of determination hadn't softened one bit. Sighing, she rose from the table and began to clear it. Something was going to have to happen pretty soon. This couldn't go on much longer. Kimmie had to eat.

"We've got a plan." Joe and Rusty stood in the doorway of the family room, looking pleased with themselves.

"We're going out to the old water hole to see the animals," Rusty told her, his dark eyes sparkling with excitement. "It's a place where Joe used to go when he was a kid."

"Joe?" she asked, raising an eyebrow, but Rusty had already run off to tell Kimmie about the planned expedition.

"I told him to call me that," Joe explained, leaning against the doorjamb and watching her. "I wanted to be something closer than a 'Mr.'"

"Oh, really?" Turning, she gave him an appraising look. "And why is that?"

"Why do I want to get closer to him?"

She nodded slowly, her arms folded across her chest. "What exactly is the point?"

He hesitated, not really sure himself. "Because I like him," he said at last, a bit defensively. "He's a great kid."

"I know that." Frustration laced with a touch of anger made her voice tremble just a bit. "But he doesn't need you to break his heart."

"Break his heart?" Joe looked bewildered. "Damn it, Chynna, I just wanted to be friendly. I'm not trying to...to..."

She stared at him, then relented a bit and gave him a half smile. "I know that. You mean well. You're a nice person." She turned away, shaking her head. She'd been alone with her children for so long, and she'd watched their needs go unmet much too often. How could she make Joe understand?

She turned back and gazed into his eyes. "But don't you see what this could do to Rusty? He doesn't have a father and he so desperately wants one."

He wasn't going to give in to this psychological

analysis. Stubbornly, he said, "Look, all I did was tell him to call me Joe."

"Okay." She held her hand up to stop the subject in its tracks. "Okay."

He shifted his weight restlessly. "Can we still go out to the water hole?"

"Sure."

"Good."

He sounded relieved, and she couldn't help but smile at him. She turned, pointing out the stack of old magazines. "I brought these back in. Since they aren't really yours, I guess they're not yours to throw away. Shall I put them in the bedroom?"

He hesitated, stealing a glance at the cover of the top item. "Uh...no, why not just leave them here?"

She made a face. "Because I don't want the kids to see them."

"Here." He looked around, then picked up the lot of them and shoved them into a cabinet. "Now they're gone. Out of sight, out of mind."

Unfortunately, the cabinet was not secure. His words had barely completed their echo in the hallway before the cabinet door flew open again, and the magazines came spilling out all over the floor, some of the most blatant pictures making a return engagement to the space between the two of them. They both stared down for a moment, then looked up and met each other's gaze.

"Back in sight, back in mind," she murmured, biting back a laugh as she sank down to sit on the couch.

He was still embarrassed by them, and that made her want to grin all the more. She watched while he bent down and began to scoop them up. Reaching out, she picked up one with a picture of a woman with the

largest breasts she'd ever seen—both quite naked and
being projected toward the cameraman as though they
were turrets on a big gun and the enemy was at hand.
Studying it for a moment, she shook her head.

"Why do men like that sort of thing?" she asked,
just making conversation. "You know, I really don't
get it."

He had most of the magazines back up in a pile and
he glanced over to see what she was looking at, then
looked away again very quickly. "That's as it should
be," he said evenly. "You're a woman. You're not
supposed to get it."

She leaned forward, her chin in her hand, and
frowned at him. "But what do you get out of it? I
mean, a nice-looking man is fun to look at for a minute
or two, but I can't imagine buying a whole magazine
full of them and looking for hours. What a waste of
time."

He snatched the offending magazine away from her
and put it on the bottom of the stack.

"You see," he said wisely, "that's because in the
grand scheme of things, when it comes to stimulation,
men are visual."

She watched him trying to jam the magazines back
in the cabinet with amusement. "And what are
women?"

He didn't look at her. He was concentrating on his
job. "I don't know."

"I do. Women are sensible."

He got the last of the magazines in and slammed
the door shut, turning the key in the lock, then stood
back and waited to see what would happen. Nothing,
it seemed. Finally, he turned to look at her.

"Women are a complete mystery to me," he told

her breezily. "But I must admit I feel a strange, mystical attraction to them."

She grinned at him. "No kidding. How unique."

"You think so?" He pretended to preen in the long mirror that decorated the far wall.

She threw a throw pillow at him, and he laughed, ducking it, but tackling her as she tried to get away, pulling her back down onto the couch in his arms. The moment was ripe with provocation, but he hesitated, and so did she. Their gazes clung together for a long ten seconds, and then the moment had passed, and they slowly, reluctantly, drew apart.

"Get ready," he told her as he rose and started for the doorway. "We're going to the watering hole."

"What should I bring?" she called after him.

"A canteen. Maybe some snacks. And a jacket. It'll be cold before we get back."

She nodded to herself very slowly. "Cold," she whispered to the air. "And very lonely."

Seven

"**W**hy do you call this a water hole?" Chynna asked him a little over an hour later as they trudged down the hill into the valley that held their destination. "It looks like a small lake."

"It is. But when we were kids, Greg and I saw some documentary on water holes out on the Serengeti Plain, and it worked just like this place does. At nightfall, all the animals for miles came to the water hole to drink. And the same thing happens here."

"Except you don't have any nightfall," she said, looking at the brilliant sky.

"Sure, we do. It's just longer and more drawn out." He kept moving, surveying for a good picnic area. "We'll go down to the edge in a bit. You'll be surprised at what we'll see."

They'd come out of the trees into the valley. A small river ran down the center of it, emptying into the lake, and a series of waterfalls let water back into the river at the far end of the body of water. Chynna fell in love with the area at first sight.

"Paradise," she whispered to herself as she put down the picnic basket on a flat rock and began to help Joe spread out the blanket. A hawk flew by, and birds sang in the trees. The rushing of the water seemed to mirror the flow of clouds across the sky. The children began to run and play in the meadow, running over tufts of jade green grass, falling among cascades of tiny yellow-and-blue flowers, poking at stashes of snow that still lingered in the shady nooks and crannies.

"Look," Rusty said, pointing at a puddle. "Something's moving." He bent over and stared into the water with Kimmie right behind him.

"Pollywogs," Joe told him. "Tadpoles. They'll be frogs pretty soon."

And sure enough, a battalion of tiny frogs began to hop out of the puddle, making the children scream, first with surprise, then with delight. Chynna watched while Joe helped them catch a few and gave them safety tips, showing them how to hold the tiny animals without hurting them, and then release them again into their natural environment.

She smiled as he came up to join her on the blanket. "It must have been wonderful growing up here," she noted.

He slumped beside her and frowned, considering. "Looking back, I guess it was pretty good. Better than concrete and drive-by shootings. But it wasn't perfect."

"No?" She glanced at him sideways. "Why not?"

He started to say something, then caught himself

and growled at her. "Oh, no, you don't, Mrs. Freud. You're not going to get me to unburden the painful experiences of my childhood so that you can pick my psyche apart."

"Aw, come on," she teased. "Be a good sport. It'll be fun."

"For you, maybe." He gave her a half grin, looking up into the low sun and noting the way the sunbeams shot out around her head like a halo. "Anyway, I'm not the one who put my picture in a catalog so that I could marry some stranger. You're the one we ought to be analyzing. Why the hell did you do that, anyway?"

She folded her hands in her lap and went very still. "I don't know if I can make you understand."

But he had to understand. He needed to. "Give it a try," he said softly.

She hesitated, looking at him speculatively, at the way his hair fell over his forehead, at his broad, competent hands, his strong arms.

"Have you ever had anyone in your life that you loved better than yourself?" she asked him. "Have you ever cared more for the welfare of someone close to you than you did for your own comfort?"

He frowned. "Sure," he began, but then he thought for a moment and couldn't come up with anyone. He'd been about to say his mother, but that wasn't really true. Not the way she seemed to mean it. He did go out of his way to do things for his mother, but he'd never been forced to make a choice that would put him at a disadvantage. He couldn't honestly say that he'd experienced what Chynna was asking him to consider.

"I guess not really," he admitted. "Not yet."

She nodded. "You don't have children," she told him. "Once you have your own children, you'll know what I mean and why I did what I did." She looked at him for a moment and decided to tell him a bit more. "I'll tell you what finally made up my mind to take the chance. Rusty has a slight learning disability, and I knew they would never help him in the schools where we lived, not the way he needed to be helped. I knew I could do a better job teaching him at home. I'm the one who cares if he learns or not. And at the same time, Kimmie was having problems at the day-care center where I was leaving her while I went to work. She's so shy, the other kids were teasing her and she...well, she just wasn't doing well."

He looked out at where Kimmie was playing and felt the urge to protect her. If he, hardly knowing her, had that urge, what must Chynna feel like?

"The problems seemed to build up day after day. And I couldn't see any solutions. I spent so much time at work, worrying all the time about what was going on with my kids...I had to find a way to make a change. You only get one chance to raise each child. You have to try to do the best for them that you can."

"Okay," he said, frowning. "I get that part. Now, here's the part I don't get. How did you get to the point where you could treat marriage like a blind date?"

She met his gaze and didn't waver. "I don't look at it quite that way," she told him levelly. "I wasn't in need of a man so much as I needed a job, and a life-style. That was what I was in the market for. And when I made an honest appraisal of my resources, I thought the only way I would have a chance of doing it well—of giving my children a better situation—was to marry someone who lived where I wanted my kids to grow up."

He stared at her, but before he could respond, the children were back, ravenously hungry and, in Rusty's case, full of stories of what they'd encountered in their trip through the meadow. He sat back and watched her with her children and wondered at a love that could be so selfless.

Oh, no, he could almost hear her whispering to him. *It's the ultimate in selfishness. Don't you see? They're part of me.*

Looking down, he met Kimmie's dispassionate gaze. He tried a smile, but she looked stern, so he gave it up pretty quickly.

"When are you going to trust me?" he asked her softly.

But she didn't have an answer yet, so he shrugged and ate his sandwich.

Chynna saw the look pass between them and she bit her lip. She knew, deep in her heart, that they could become close with the right circumstances. What she didn't know was when that might happen—how long it would take. And there wasn't much time. Very soon, Joe was going to walk out of their lives.

Could she let that happen? She didn't have a whole lot of choice. If only she could think of some way to hold him, to make him want to stay. She'd never known a man who seemed so right for her and her family. If she could have picked a man out of a catalog, and had waited for the perfect one to come along, it would have been Joe. They said women often fell in love with the wrong men. Here she was feeling very much on the verge of falling for the perfect man—and it didn't really matter. She wasn't going to be allowed to have a real chance at him, was she?

She didn't have much time. If she was going to devise a battle plan, she'd better do so quickly. Sitting back, she watched him and wondered.

When the food was devoured and the basket packed away, Joe gathered them all together for the trek down to the water.

"You've got to be very quiet," he told the children as they walked along. "If the animals hear you, they won't come near."

Their side of the river was lined with thick brush, and the other side had trees coming down almost to the water, but no brush to speak of. Joe led them into a thicket where they settled and sat quietly, parting the branches with their hands and waiting to see animals come to drink on the other side.

"I don't see any," Rusty said in a loud stage whisper, after watching for about thirty seconds.

"Be patient," Joe whispered back. "We just arrived like a conquering army driving elephants across the land. They'll have heard us. They'll be wary for a while. We'll have to wait until they think we're gone for sure."

They waited another five minutes, and just when the kids were beginning to fidget again, there was a sound on the other side. They sat very still, holding their breaths. A rustling was heard in the trees, and then a beautiful blacktail deer came from the woods, stepping carefully, nose up for danger. She stopped for a moment and sniffed the air, then stepped toward the water, and from behind her came a fawn, a quarter her size and dappled where she was tan. It scampered past her and made its way to the bank while she moved with a more stately pace. They both began to drink, the mother raising her head every few seconds, checking for threats from up the valley, then down.

Joe glanced down at Chynna and the kids. Each seemed to be holding a breath, watching with wide eyes. Kimmie's thumb had dropped out of her mouth. She was staring at the deer with all her might, her mouth slightly open, her eyes big as saucers. Warmed, he looked back at the animals, and he had to admit, he felt almost as thrilled with the sight as the others did. All his years in suburban southern California had dulled him to this sort of experience, and now he felt as though he were awakening to it again. This was real. This was Alaska.

It wasn't until the deer had retreated into the woods again that anyone spoke. Rusty and Chynna were brimming with reaction, but Kimmie didn't say a thing, and Joe leaned down to catch her attention.

"Did you like that, Kimmie?" he asked her, and she looked up at him solemnly, took her thumb and very carefully, deliberately, popped it back into her mouth. He had to laugh. She'd decided he wasn't to be tolerated, and she meant it.

But he was growing more and more determined to break open that little ice-cube heart, and he meant it, too.

Another sound came from the opposite bank, this one louder than the first, and they lapsed into silence again, staring out and waiting. Joe was hoping for a fox, or maybe a small brown bear, but when a horse with rider came into view, everyone in the thicket heaved a sigh of disappointment.

The rider seemed to hear them as he loosened the reins and let his horse drink. At any rate, he spotted them in the brush and tipped his hat. "Howdy," he called out.

Joe rose and nodded to the man, and the others followed him, stepping out so that they could be seen. The rider was a clean-shaved, handsome man in his thirties, dressed in buckskin with fringe that blew in the breeze and a wide-brimmed hat that shaded his face. He looked sharply at the party across the body of water and seemed to know who they were.

"Say," he called out to Joe. "You the fella's got an extra woman on his hands?"

Joe's head came up, and Chynna gasped softly.

"No," Joe said, his voice gruff. "You must have me mixed up with someone else."

The man frowned. "You're Joe Camden, ain't you?"

Joe nodded slowly.

"Well, then you're the one," he noted, sliding down off his horse and coming to the edge of the water. "And if that's the woman you're trying to get a place for, I would take kindly to being introduced."

Joe turned and looked at Chynna. She looked back with panic in her eyes. It had been kind of funny and flattering to hear that men were around offering to take her if one of the Camden men didn't want her, but to come face-to-face with it was something else again. The man was clean and handsome, and still, going off with him like this would be madness, and she knew it. She stared at Joe, shaking her head imperceptibly, and wondered what he was going to do.

Joe searched her eyes, then turned back to the man. "You're too late, buddy," he told him. "I've decided I do want her after all."

The man nodded. "I can see why," he noted. "But

say, if she's got any sisters, send one of them my way. I need a wife bad. I've been lonely too long.''

Joe met Chynna's relieved glance and grinned at her, feeling suddenly lighthearted and particularly friendly to the man.

"There are other women," he noted.

"Not around here there aren't."

Joe frowned, knowing he was pretty near right. "If you want a woman that badly, why don't you go ask that woman named Nancy?" he suggested. "I hear she's a looker."

"Nancy?" The man grunted as he began gathering up his horse's reins in his hand. "That little gal who does nails?" He shook his head and swung back up into the saddle. "No, thanks. I went in and got myself a pedicure, and she darn near talked my ear off. She's got a sharp tongue, does Nancy. A man should think twice before saddling himself with a wife's got a sharp tongue. That's like signing up for a season in hell."

"You got that right," Joe called back.

They stood on the bank and watched as the man began to ride away, Chynna watching the scene in amazement—mostly wondering why the explicit sexism of the situation, why the exaggerated maleness of the environment—didn't bother her more. Back in Chicago, she would have protested their assumptions. But somehow, it seemed right and fitting out here in this wilderness. Fitting, and comfortable.

Once the man was out of sight, Joe turned back to Chynna, shaking his head and looking her up and down.

"The man just wanted to look you over," he told her, leashing his amusement as best he could. "He was in the market for a wife and he thought you might do.'' He grinned, then bit it back, while she gagged. ''Now, tell me why that bothered you so much?'' he asked her. ''How was that much different from signing up with an agency and taking a stranger who writes to you to be your husband?''

She thought for a moment. ''Because I got to participate in the choosing,'' she said at last. ''That was very different.''

Before he could respond, a shout turned them around. Suddenly, they realized that the children were no longer with them. Rusty was running toward the far end of the little lake, and as they looked, they saw something else in the water.

Chynna gasped, her hand to her throat. ''Kimmie!'' she cried. ''She fell in!'' Then she was running, stumbling over twigs and fallen branches, trying to get to her baby.

Joe had seen her, too. Her little head was bobbing, and she'd been caught up by the current. She was headed for the falls.

He didn't have to think; he just reacted. Running alongside the water, he began stripping off clothing, and by the time he'd almost caught up to where she was, he was down to jeans and socks. Without a moment's hesitation, he dived into the icy water and swam strongly toward her. In seconds, she was in his arms.

''Hold on, Kimmie,'' he called out, grabbing her away from the rocks. ''Hold me tightly. I've got you, but you've got to hold on.''

She did, clinging to him like a burr, and he worked against the current, fighting the strong pull toward the falls. The water was horribly cold, numbing, and he began to lose feeling in his feet. But he went on. There

was no choice. He had to go on, or Kimmie would be
badly hurt.

They struggled, fighting for land. The cold and the
sweep of the river worked against them, and Joe
cursed the fact that he wasn't in as good shape as he
could have been. He had to hold Kimmie with one
arm and swim with the other. There were flashes of
fear when he wondered if he would get her back in
good shape. But finally, the bank was in reach, and he
pulled up on the sandy shore, panting, exhausted, lying
on the ground with his eyes closed.

Chynna and Rusty were there, saying things, touching him, trying to check Kimmie out to see if she was
hurt. But she wouldn't let go. Her little arms were
around his neck, and she wouldn't release them. The
more they pulled, the more tightly she clung, until
finally he'd caught his breath and revived enough to
sit up and gently pry her away.

They went back to the house as quickly as they
could, and Chynna gave Kimmie a warm bath and
wrapped her tightly in warm clothes. She had a few
cuts, a few bruises, but otherwise she seemed to be all
right. Joe had a gash over one eye and a couple of
pulled muscles, but he was fine. When he went in to
say good-night to Kimmie, her thumb was back in her
mouth and she followed his every movement with her
dark-eyed gaze, but she still wouldn't talk to him. He
left disappointed and beginning to think there was no
way to reach her.

"Thank you," Chynna told him when both children
were in bed and they were alone. "I can't tell you
how much..." Her voice choked, and he drew her
close, patting her awkwardly before he drew away
again.

"It's no big deal," he said. *I would do just about anything for that little girl,* he could have added, but he didn't. Still, he realized it was true. He couldn't stand her silence, and her huge eyes haunted him. If he could have thought of some way to win her over, make her smile just once, he would do it, regardless of what it took.

Still, he was glad she seemed to be basically unhurt. He wandered the house restlessly while Chynna cleaned up the kids' toys, telling himself he was anxious to get going. Once he had Chynna and the children out of the house and on their way, Greg would probably appear in the yard, and he could get on with the errand that had brought him here. His mother's birthday was days away, and he wanted to make sure Greg came to see her for it. Nobody had been able to persuade him to come to Anchorage yet. This time, Joe was determined.

But first, they had to get through the night. He ran a hand through his hair and swore softly at himself. He was making this whole thing more difficult than it needed to be and he knew it. It would be so much easier if Chynna wasn't...if she weren't so...if he could only stop thinking about what it would be like to take her to bed.

There. He'd admitted it to himself. She was driving him crazier than a june bug on Memorial Day. The curve of her cheek, the way her hair flew out around her face, the scent she left behind in the room when she left it, everything was eating at him. He could hardly stand it.

"What's the name of that perfume you're wearing?" he asked grumpily as she walked past, picking up the children's toys.

"Perfume?" She straightened and smiled. "I call it good old soap and water."

"You're kidding." He frowned, annoyed and not sure if it was at her or at himself. "Then how does your scent last in the air like that?" he asked begrudgingly.

"Magic," she told him with an impish grin.

"Magic," he repeated under his breath as he watched her sway from the room. That had to be it. Otherwise, why would he be feeling so nuts?

He had to get back to L.A., back to the life he knew, back to things he was used to. He had friends there, his job. No girlfriend lately, but that was just because he'd grown tired of dating empty-headed starlets and success-hungry lawyers. It seemed all he met were from one group or the other. What he needed was a nice woman who had brains and a metabolism about half that of your average hummingbird. A little class would be nice. Maybe a caring personality. A pretty face. Someone very much like...

No. He wasn't going to say it, not even to himself. Chynna was great, but she wasn't his dream girl. How could she be? Dream girls didn't come with two little kids clinging to their legs. And anyway, she was supposed to marry his brother.

Not that he had any intention of letting that happen. But still, ethics were ethics.

A glance out the window told him she was outside, leaning on the fence and staring at the mountains. He went out the front door and swung across the porch, coming up behind her and looking at what she must be seeing.

"It is beautiful," he acknowledged, as though he knew she was going to tell him so any second and wanted to beat her to it. "And deadly. You know how many men die up there every year?"

She nodded slowly. "So you aren't one of those who think beauty is worth dying for," she said.

He gave a short laugh. "Listen, you want to see beauty, you ought to get a look at the beach at Malibu on a sunny spring afternoon."

Chynna looked at him over her shoulder. "Lots of itsy-bitsy teeny-weeny bikinis?" she guessed.

He pretended outrage at her suggestion. "I was talking about the sunlight on the water," he told her. "And the view of Catalina on the horizon."

She grinned. "Oops. I stand corrected."

He moved next to her and leaned beside her. Their shoulders were almost touching. The mountains stood out against the liquid blue sky, a silhouette of power and majesty that tended to take your breath away. Neither one of them spoke for a long moment.

"Makes you feel sort of small, doesn't it?" she said at last.

He blinked, realizing suddenly that she'd hit the nail on the head. That was exactly why he'd been so hot to get out of Alaska when he was young. He had to find a place where the landscape didn't dwarf you, where expectations were kept to human size. So he'd picked southern California, which had its own laundry list of intimidating circumstances—but they were all new to him, and he'd prevailed over them in time. He'd done well. He had a good job making good money, living in a beautiful area, with all the perks that came with the good life. Everything was perfect, damn it! So why did he feel like snarling?

"So tell me, Mr. Joe Camden," Chynna said, when he'd been silent too long and she had to say something, "how have you managed to reach this point in your life without getting shanghaied into marriage somewhere along the way?"

"I live in L.A., remember? It's not exactly a marrying town, at least not the part I live in."

She looked toward the white clouds scudding across the sky. "You could always move," she noted quietly.

He turned to look at her and tried to grin, though it felt as forced as it probably looked. "Not if it made me more vulnerable to marriage. What would be the point?"

She faced him and almost smiled. "How silly of me. Well, then, it seems you've chosen the perfect place to live. You must be very happy."

"I am happy." He sounded defensive and he knew it, but once the words were out, he couldn't take them back, nor could he modulate the tone.

But she was smiling, as though she knew she'd touched a nerve and was glad to have done so. "Well, you don't have to bite my head off," she said mildly.

"I wasn't."

"My mistake." She grinned like a woman who'd won the last point in a tennis match. "It must be that all that happiness beaming out from you that blinded me to the truth."

He glared at her helplessly. Why was it so hard to get through to her? And why was it bothering him so much that she continued to laugh at him this way?

"Listen, I'm living the way I want to live."

She nodded, acknowledging his point, but that didn't stop her. "You really don't think you'll ever want a real home, with children and all that goes with it?" Catching the look on his face, she laughed, patting him on the arm. "Don't look so scared. I'm not trying to trap you into anything. I'm just concerned about you.''

''About me? Hey, we're just two proverbial ships passing in the night. What do you care about what happens to me?''

She stared at him for a long moment, wondering if she were wrong about him, wondering where the real soul of Joe Camden was hidden. It was obvious he didn't feel the same bond growing between them that she did, and she looked away, hiding the slight tremor in her smile. She'd had hopes. But prospects looked fairly dim at the moment. He was bound and determined not to fall in love, wasn't he? And she wasn't going to have time to work on changing his mind.

''I just have a natural urge to nurture, I guess,'' she said lightly.

But he wasn't listening any longer. Her hair had brushed his face as she turned, her scent, perfumed or not, was drowning him and he could hardly breathe.

''What happened to the kids' father?'' he asked abruptly. ''Were you married to him?''

She glanced down at her hand and saw, with a start, that her ring finger was empty. Of course, she knew that. She'd taken off the ring before she'd left Chicago. After all, if she was going to marry someone new, it wouldn't do to arrive with the first husband's brand still on her, so to speak. But she wasn't used to the nakedness yet, and it still gave her a shock when she noticed it.

''I was married to him,'' she answered calmly. ''We went together from our junior year in high school on and were married right out of college.''

''Young love,'' he muttered, hoping he didn't sound

as jealous as he felt, and at the same time, shocked at himself for feeling that way.

"It was," she said simply. "We had Rusty and Kimmie and were very happy for as long as it lasted."

"And what broke up that old gang of yours?"

"Kevin died."

"Oh. Sorry." He winced, wishing he could take back this feeling of frustrated anger. He wasn't even sure what it was or whom he was angry with, but he knew he was acting like a jerk, and he couldn't seem to shake it. "How did it happen?"

"He died in a car accident." She paused, steeled herself, and added, "He'd been drinking."

Joe thought immediately of the look on her face when she'd found the bottle beside his bed, and suddenly his anger turned toward this much loved Kevin, a man who would risk losing his life and leave a family like this, a woman like Chynna, kids like Rusty and Kimmie, alone in the world, all for the sake of a drink.

He wanted to comfort her, but the set of her shoulders told him she wasn't asking for solace and wouldn't necessarily welcome it should it come. Everything about her was sending signals, beating a rhythm in his blood, making his brain go fuzzy.

It had been a long time since a woman had sent him into this sort of tailspin. Eighth grade might have been the last time, when he'd walked Elinor Bingley home from the junior-high dance, his palms sweaty as he planned how he was going to kiss her. First, he was going to casually lean over her as they stopped to try out the echo at the empty old brick brewery, but she started to teach him how to whistle between two fingers and he got sidetracked and forgot. Then he planned to pull her back just before the pothole on the corner, saving her from the mud and grabbing a quick kiss at the same time. But she dashed ahead of him and sailed over the pothole, leaving him, off balance, to catch the edge and splash mud all over his best slacks. Under the single town streetlight, behind the bleachers at the baseball diamond, even on her front steps, every plan fell through for one reason or another, and he'd just about given up when he heard her father's gruff voice and heavy tread as he made his way to the front door to let his daughter in. But Elinor gave him a cocky grin, reached up and planted her lips full on his, and even held it for a count or two, before darting away and disappearing inside her house, leaving him alone on the front porch.

He could still remember the flush of absolute joy. "I did it," he'd muttered to himself, flush with triumph.

"Fooling myself even then," he muttered now, realizing it was Elinor who had done it, not he.

"What?" Chynna asked, catching the tail end of his statement.

He turned and stared at her, studying every curve of her face, the light glow of her cheek, the way her eyelashes shaded eyes that sparkled like spring snow on the lake.

"I'm going to have to kiss you one more time," he told her distractedly, taking her by the shoulders and frowning down into her face.

"Why?" she asked solemnly, her eyes huge, her heart beating and hope rising in her chest.

He grimaced. Her mouth looked soft and warm and full and damn near irresistible. "Mostly so I won't

want to so much anymore,'' he told her honestly. "So
I'll stop thinking about it."

She met his gaze and searched it. "You really think
that's going to work?" she asked him softly.

"No," he admitted, his fingers tightening on her
shoulders. "But I can't think of anything else to do."

"Okay," she whispered, raising her arms and slipping them around his neck so that her body molded
itself to his. "Let's give it a try."

So he did. He meant for it to be quick and clean, a
good, solid kiss that would tell him she was like any
other woman, that the lingering effects of the other
kisses they'd shared lived mostly in his mind and
imagination, that he'd been dreaming. But he knew
right away that he'd been trying to fool himself again.

Only this time, it wouldn't work. He was under the
spell of her magic, like a bug in a spider's web, and
the more he twisted and turned and tried to free himself, the more he was wrapping himself in the silken
threads that would bind him forever if he didn't watch
out.

A cool breeze sprang up, blowing across their faces,
but her mouth was so warm, he hardly noticed anything else. He was sinking into her, letting her pull
him in and take him with her, sailing on that breeze,
holding her so that he wouldn't fall, so that she would
stay afloat, so that they both could share in the glide
that might never end.

He wanted her, and yet he'd wanted women before
and it had never been like this. He wanted to plunge
inside her and take the sweet pleasure her body could
give him, but at the same time, he had a strange urge
to hold her high, like an offering to a sun god, like
something to be guarded and cherished. He wanted to

own her. There was no other way to put it. He wanted to take possession, body and soul, and make her his own.

And that was plain insanity, because she wasn't his and could never be. She'd come to marry his brother. He had no right to her, and couldn't have had her in any case. She was off-limits, and here he was kissing her again.

He drew back slowly, because she was so good and it was so damn hard to resist her. She looked at him coolly, as though she had hardly been affected by what had happened between them, and she said in a calm, clear voice, "What's the verdict?"

He gazed at her groggily, his sense still whirling. "Wh-what?"

"On the kissing cure." Reaching up, she touched his face with the flat of her hand for a split second, then drew away, confusing him again. "Did it render you immune to my charms?" she asked, teasing him.

He stared at her for a moment, clearing his mind, then swore softly and obscenely and turned away.

"We can't do this anymore," he said gruffly, as though set to take action. "We've got to forget this ever happened."

She laughed softly, but managed an innocent look. "Forget that what ever happened?" she asked, her eyes wide.

He frowned and waved a hand. "The kiss..." he began, then saw the look on her face. "Oh, I get it." He half smiled. "I'm slow, but I do get there eventually."

She wanted to answer that, to tease him again, bait him, cajole him, even flirt a little, but she held off, knowing it wouldn't be fair. He was trying so hard to be honorable, and she had to respect that. Much as she regretted it, they weren't a match made in heaven. That was just not to be. He'd tried to tell her again and again, and she might as well let the lesson sink in. He wasn't going to marry anyone, and much as she was attracted to him, much as she respected him and thought he might just be the one—without marriage, a relationship of any kind would be impossible. She had children to think of. If it just wasn't going to be, it was best they hold back and try to forget it, just as he'd demanded.

She left the fence and started back toward the house, moving toward security, but he stopped her with a hand on her arm.

"You know, I haven't given you the details yet. I should have told you before. I've got you a ride back to Anchorage tomorrow."

There. He'd said it. Bracing himself, he looked down into her eyes, but to his surprise, her face was serene and she was almost smiling.

"Cancel it," she said calmly. "I'm not leaving."

"What?"

"Don't worry," she told him, just in case he thought she meant to latch on to him for the duration. "We'll have to stay here tonight, but after that, we won't be imposing upon your hospitality any longer."

He was gazing at her as though she'd proposed contacting space aliens and planning a get-acquainted dinner party. "Where will you go? What are you going to do?"

She turned and looked him square in the eye, like the professional woman she meant to become. "Don't worry. I've laid the groundwork. I've got some money saved, and Annie is going to help me. She knows of a place I can rent with a storefront and living space in the back.''

He was gazing at her in complete bewilderment. He still didn't have a clue as to what she was talking about. She took a deep breath and came out with the coup de grâce.

"I'm going to look into starting a business."

"A business? In Dunmovin?" He blinked, stunned. "You're kidding. What sort of business?"

She licked her lips and told him. "A coffee bar." Holding her breath, she waited for his response.

It took a minute. At first, he didn't seem to understand. But then realization dawned in his eyes. "A coffee bar?" He stared at her, appalled. "Oh, now I've heard everything."

Her chin rose and her jaw tightened. "Why not?"

"A coffee bar?" His chuckle held more disdain than humor. "These people won't drink cappuccinos and lattes. They want beer and they want it thick and dark as molasses."

She tossed her head, turning from him and beginning to walk toward the house. "This is almost the twenty-first century, you know," she reminded him over her shoulder. "I think you'll find that times, they are a-changin'." Turning back, she found he'd followed her, and she set her hands on her hips. "Besides, I won't just make coffees. I'll make sandwiches, too. I'll fix pack lunches for the men going out to hunt and fish, and the men going out to work on the pipeline, and…"

He was shaking his head in astonishment and finally he couldn't contain his comments. "Maybe I'm the one who's nuts, but I can't see those big burly men coming into your shop for a quick mocha with whipped cream and picking up an avocado-and-alfalfa-sprout sandwich to take up into the mountains with them.''

He shook his head. ''Chynna, I know these men. I grew up here. They don't act like men in the city, because they don't like the city. They like the wilderness and they want to act like wild men. You're not going to tame them.''

A stubborn light shone in her dark eyes. ''We'll see.''

He hesitated, wanting to stop her, as though she were walking too near the edge of a cliff and he was the one who could grab her back away from danger, wanting to shield her from pain. ''You're going to end up with a broken heart,'' he warned.

''Maybe.'' She stopped, thought for a moment, then turned back and told him what she thought in no uncertain terms. ''And maybe I'll end up with a business that makes enough of a living to make it possible to keep my children out here in this beautiful, clean and healthy place. And maybe I'll be able to do all that without having to sell myself in marriage to some man I don't love.''

That shut him up, and as she flounced away, he watched her go and found himself chuckling softly. Well, maybe so. If all it took was pure guts and determination, she would have it made. Maybe so.

Eight

Chynna woke and found herself in darkness. For just a moment, she thought she was back in the apartment in Chicago, and every muscle tensed. Then she remembered. Alaska. Suddenly, the bed felt softer, the air lighter, the sounds of crickets reassuring. Yes, she loved it here. She had to stay.

But something had woken her. What was it? Had one of the children called to her?

She lay very quietly for a moment, but there was no sound. Still, something wasn't quite right. She could sense it.

Slipping out of bed, she padded into the hallway and pushed open the door to the room where the children were sleeping. Rusty's head lay on his pillow, and his eyes were closed, a picture of peace and tranquillity. But Kimmie's side of the bed was empty.

"Kimmie?" she whispered, glancing around the room. "Where are you, honey?"

She looked up and down the hall, then made her way through the darkened living room to the kitchen, where she switched on the light. No Kimmie. Her heart began to beat just a little faster, and her steps were more hurried as she moved through the house, turning on lights as she went.

"Kimmie?" she called in a normal voice.

Memories of the wolf howl from the night before came creeping into her mind, and she shook them away. Kimmie wouldn't go outside. Would she? She hurried on through the house, searching, dreading....

What if she had gone outside? What if she'd been looking for her mother and lost her way and ended up outside, alone and frightened. What if...?

Finally, there was only one room left to look in. Walking quickly to the end of the hallway, she found that Joe's door was ajar and she pushed it open. The light from the hallway fell into the room, and there on the floor, at the foot of the bed, on a little round rug, lay Kimmie, her eyes closed, her thumb in her mouth.

Chynna drew in her breath, and her eyes filled with tears of relief. For just a moment, she stood there, giving thanks that she'd found her baby unharmed, but also taking in the atmosphere. Joe was sound asleep, lying on his side with his arm around his pillow. And there was Kimmie, at the foot of his bed, as close as she dared get to him, with her blanket clutched to her chest and her stuffed koala bear in one arm. Chynna laughed softly, and all her love was in her eyes as she watched her baby sleep.

But she couldn't stay there forever, watching. She was going to have to pick Kim up and carry her back to her own bed. Still, she hated to have Joe miss this. She hesitated. Would he care? But this was too good, too cute. She had to share it. It had been so long since she'd had someone to share things like this with, it would be wonderful to have the closeness, even if just for tonight.

"Joe." She put a hand on his bare shoulder, and he rolled onto his back, his eyes wide open.

"Chynna?" For a moment, he thought he was dreaming. She was leaning over him, her hair sweeping down and tickling his bare chest. Could this be real? But then her scent filled his head, and he knew she was really there. He reached out to pull her down into his arms, but she was laughing softly and avoiding his embrace.

"I didn't come in here to seduce you," she whispered, batting his hand away. "Come here. I want you to see something."

He rose sleepily, hitching up the drooping pajama bottoms he wore, but when he saw what she'd called him to see, he was suddenly wide-awake.

"Kimmie," he said in a stage whisper. "How did she get here?"

Chynna smiled at him. "She came on her own. She snuck in during the night. I was looking all over the house for her, and finally I came into your room...."

He frowned, bewildered. "But why would she come in here? She hates me."

Chynna shook her head, her gaze softening as she looked at him. "She adores you, you idiot. She's just afraid to show it."

Her eyes were telling him more than he wanted to know, and he looked down at the child. Females were hard to read, no matter what the age. But if Chynna said Kimmie liked him, that was enough for him. Reaching down, he scooped her up into his arms, koala bear and all. "I guess we'd better put you back in your bed," he told her softly.

She surfaced for a second or two, pushing her way through the cloud of sleep, her dark eyes blinking in the pale light. Then she put her arms around his neck, holding on tightly, and when her head fell against his chest, she was out again, secure in his arms, happy, it seemed. Joe swallowed hard and felt a lump grow in his throat.

"Come on," Chynna said, leading the way. "Let's put her down."

She watched him, saw how tenderly he held her child, and something broke open inside her and suddenly she knew, as though someone had spoken the words, that this was the man she wanted. This was the man who was slipping through her fingers.

But there was something else. As she watched him, she knew there was more. She was in love with Joe Camden. Far beyond how good he would be for her children, how perfect a match they could make, she was in love with him. Head over heels like she'd only been once before. What was she prepared to do about it? Nothing? Standing back, she bit her lip and felt the stirrings of a pain that was to come.

Joe removed Kimmie from his arms reluctantly. She felt so good there. An angel. That was what she looked like when he put her back in her bed and pulled the covers up around her. He looked down at her, and something hurt in his chest, and suddenly he was backing away. He had to get out of here, get away from these kids. If he didn't watch out...if he didn't watch it...

He didn't put into words what he was afraid would happen, but he knew what it was and he knew how to avoid it. Get away from these kids, get Chynna out of town and go back to L.A. and the life he'd been living for all these years. Get back to normal. That was all there was to it. Should be easy.

All he had to do was get past Chynna in the hallway, get into his own bed, go to sleep and in the morning things would be calm again. He could handle that, couldn't he?

Closing the door to the children's room, he turned and saw exactly why that scenario wasn't going to work out quite as efficiently as he'd projected. Chynna stood between him and his room, her hair down around her shoulders in a golden haze, the light from behind her shining through her sheer nightgown, outlining her slender curves. He took a ragged breath and steeled himself to resist.

"We'd better get some sleep," he said, starting to edge past her. "We still have to discuss what you're going to do."

She stood very still, not giving him any ground. "There's no discussion needed," she said simply. "The children and I are moving into the place Annie has to rent. You don't have to worry about us any longer."

He hesitated, knowing he should move on, knowing to stay and argue was pointless, and more likely dangerous. But he had to say it.

"You can't stay here in Dunmovin," he told her earnestly. "It's crazy. It won't work."

She sighed, shaking her head. "Why not let us sink or swim? What do you care?" she asked him softly.

"You won't be here. You'll be going back to Los Angeles."

There was a buzzing in his head. She was too close, and her scent was too strong. He couldn't avoid seeing the way the fabric of her nightgown clung to her breasts, and it was making him light-headed.

"Do you want to come with me to L.A.?" he heard himself asking, to his own dismay. "There are more jobs there lately and…"

What was he saying? Was he out of his mind? And yet, he couldn't stop. Something inside was coming out, as though he had no will of his own.

"…and I could help you find a place to live and a job with a good day-care center."

But she wouldn't take the bait. That wasn't what she wanted at all, and she wasn't ready to settle yet.

"No," she told him firmly. "In Los Angeles, I would run into the same problems I had in Chicago. This is the best place for us. Right here in Alaska."

He was conscious of her nearness and of his own nakedness, except for the baggy pajama bottoms that hung low on his hips. He thought he could feel her warm breath on his skin, and it sent his senses spinning.

"Why do you want to stay?" he asked her, no longer thinking about what he was saying, just making sound to try to cover up the way he was reacting to her. "Are you still hoping Greg will want to marry you when he shows up?"

Her head came up, and she stared into his eyes, her own eyes dark pools in the dim light of the hallway. "Greg has made it very clear that he's not really interested in marriage," she told him softly. "I think we've moved beyond that, don't you?"

He didn't know what she meant, but it hardly mattered. He stood very still, frozen by the electricity in her dark, velvet gaze. She was so beautiful. What had she said earlier? That he wasn't prepared to die for beauty? Right now, he felt as though he could. Everything in him wanted her, wanted to take her the way a man conquered land. And yet, who was conquering whom? As he stood paralyzed, she lifted her hand and flattened it just above his heart, as though she were searching for his heartbeat. He felt the muscles of his stomach contract and he gasped, reaching up to cover her hand with his own.

"Chynna," he murmured, fighting for strength, choking out the words, "you'd better go. You'd better…"

But his words evaporated as her hand moved on his flesh, and he lost the power of speech for a moment.

"If you can give me a good reason," she told him softly, her gaze holding his, "I'll go off to bed and leave you alone. But if there's no reason…"

He grabbed her wrist and held it tightly. "You came to be my brother's wife," he said, his voice gritty. "Isn't that reason enough?"

She shook her head slowly, her gaze locked on his. "I don't know your brother," she whispered. "But I know you."

What she said didn't make a lot of sense, but it didn't have to. They both knew where this was going and they both had to agree for it to get there. He stared into her eyes and silently made a bargain. Reaching up, she pressed her palm to his cheek and kissed his lips, and his arms slowly slid around her, holding her tightly while he soaked in her warmth and held it to him. He closed his eyes and let himself feel. Words

were no longer enough to say what they needed to say
to each other. Something else would have to take their
place.

He took her to his bed, the same bed he'd slept in
all his young, growing-up life, the same bed where
he'd dreamed of girls and escape from Alaska, and
bringing her there somehow seemed to bring a closing
to his circle. Security conscious, she locked the door
to his room and made sure he had protection. Then
she slipped off her nightgown and let him glory in her
body.

Her body. He'd never seen anything so beautiful,
so lush, so smooth, so infinitely desirable. He let his
gaze follow the long line of her leg, the rounded ele-
gance of her breast with its tight, dark tip, the smooth
dip of her navel, the curve of her shoulder, the pulse
that beat at the base of her throat as her excitement
grew, and then he made the same trip with his hand,
until his breath was ragged and he had to fight to keep
from spoiling the moment.

It had been a long time since he'd wanted a woman
this badly, a long time since sex had been special. He
buried his lips in her soft skin and melted with her,
his hands molding her, his body coming down on top
of her, taking her with him on the slide into delirium.
As his instincts took over, as his maleness rose and
surged inside him, he felt a sense of power he'd never
had before. She was his. For this moment, anyway.

Lovemaking had always been pleasant but not particularly urgent to Chynna, and she expected the same
slow response this time. But as she watched him,
watched the way his desire grew as he explored her,
watched the way the light in his eyes went from ad-
miration to lust to stark, hungering need, very soon his

touch was conjuring up answering sensations that surprised her. Her flesh seemed to burn, her hips began
to move of their own accord and suddenly she wanted
him the way a drowning man wanted air. She had to
have him, have him deep and sure and strong within
her, and she made soft sounds that told him exactly
that, while her hands urged him to join her, come together in a dance as old as life itself.

He took her as though he were claiming her. That
was the way she felt it. She accepted his mastery,
needed it at that moment, knowing in her bones the
ancient irony that made his power her triumph. Deep,
deep inside, she ached to make him hers and for a
moment, just a moment, it seemed to come true, as
they spiraled higher and higher toward the sun.

I love you, she thought as their bodies clung in the
last ebb of the intensity. And it was true. She loved
him in ways she had never loved Kevin, though she
had loved Kevin with all her heart.

But this...this was something more. He'd taken her
further, higher, harder, and that was part of it. But
there was much more. She loved him with a fierce
sense of bonding, something she'd never experienced
quite this way before. She felt a part of him.

Rolling over, she looked into his eyes to see what
he was feeling, to see if he'd known what she'd experienced, if he in any way felt the same.

But his eyes were troubled, and her heart sank. He
reached out and combed his fingers through her hair,
caressing her, but his eyes didn't give back the love
she needed to feel there. Leaning down, she kissed his
shoulder, his chest, his stomach, as though kisses
could somehow make him feel it, too. But he pulled
her up to face him, and his smile was bittersweet.

"This was crazy," he told her. "You know that. Chynna, I can't promise you anything. You understand that, don't you?"

"Shh," she told him, putting a finger to her lips. "Don't talk. If all we have is tonight, I want to make the most of it." She dropped a kiss on his mouth, her hair falling down around their faces like a protective curtain. "We can talk tomorrow," she whispered. "There's a long night ahead."

He groaned and laughed softly. "How did you get to be such a vixen?" he asked her. "Somehow, that wasn't the impression I got when you first arrived. You didn't seem so bold."

She gazed down at him. "I'm not," she said, giving him a slow half grin. "I've never made love with any man other than Kevin, my husband. I was scared to death. Couldn't you tell?"

He shook his head, frowning at her in a sort of wonder. "I don't believe you're scared of anything," he told her. "You take my breath away."

She grinned. "Here." She kissed him playfully on the lips. "Have it back. You're going to need it."

He laughed and reached for her, and in a moment they were wrestling, teasing each other and reminding each other to keep the noise down, but driving each other closer and closer to desire, until it overtook them once again and they came together with a gasp on his part and small cries of delight on hers, rising once again and finding an even sweeter joy.

She woke up in the morning in her own bed and stretched, feeling luxuriously wonderful and not remembering why at first. Then she did, and the smile broke on her face, filling her body with happiness. Joe

was a wonderful man, and the night they had shared
was something no one could ever take away from her.
She had it for keeps.

And then someone cleared his throat, and all her
good feelings fled, not to return again for a long, long
time.

"Good morning," a male voice said before she'd
had a chance to finish reacting to the throat clearing.
"You must be Chynna Sinclair."

She whirled in the bed, pulling the covers up to her
chin, and gazed out at a wild-looking, very hairy man
who sat in the armchair across the room. His blue eyes
were lively, his face rather handsome even though she
couldn't see much of it because of the beard, and his
form long and lanky. He looked like a younger, wilder
version of Joe. But something was missing, and she
knew right away it was the look in the eyes. Greg's
look was slightly blank where Joe looked warm and
quick to understand.

"You must be Greg," she said, her voice cracking
with sudden stress.

"I must be," he agreed, nodding. He looked
friendly but wary, like a huge puppy dog who had
suddenly grown into his big paws and didn't quite
know how to handle that yet. "Sorry I wasn't here to
greet you when you arrived. But hey, I left the door
unlocked for you."

"I noticed."

He nodded again and looked a bit embarrassed,
glancing around the room as though looking for a new
topic of conversation. "Say, who are these kids you've
got with you?" he asked her as he thought of it.

Funny how easy it was to tell the man she was
contracted to marry about Rusty and Kim this time.

"They're my kids. I didn't tell you about them before. But they're mine."

He shrugged, obviously ready to adapt to anything. "That's cool. I always wanted kids. Now I can have them without all the work." He grinned. "Kind of like getting a dog that's already house-trained."

"Kind of like," she echoed, blinking at him groggily, still too stunned to know what to say to him.

"Hey, having kids will be fun," he went on, looking very happy about it now that he'd thought it over. "I can teach them how to ride and fish and hunt. We'll have a great time together. And you can stay home and cook the food."

Chynna blinked at him, trying to clear her mind, wondering just how old he actually was. He'd said thirty in his letter, but this young man seemed about eighteen and not too sure of how to deal with the world as yet.

"Are you sure what you want is a wife?" she asked him, letting a tiny dose of acid edge her tone. "It sounds more like you might want a mother and a couple of new siblings."

"Oh, no." He was very sure of this. "I've got a mother. She's in Anchorage. I wanted a wife because...well..." He turned beet red for a moment. "There aren't any girls around here except for Nancy, and she turned me down."

"I see." Sounded like Nancy might be one smart cookie after all. Chynna shook her head, mostly to clear it, but also in amazement. This was the man she'd come to marry. What was she, nuts?

But looking at him, she relented. He looked nice enough, even sort of endearing in a bearlike way. She shouldn't be too harsh too quickly. Maybe it was just too early to make snap judgments. Maybe she ought to give him a chance.

She glanced at her clothes on the nearby dresser and looked at the door, about to ask him to leave while she got ready to face the day, but before she had a chance to speak, Joe appeared in her doorway.

He'd pulled on jeans, but his chest was still bare, and he wore a very sexy smile when he first looked in on her, was just about to say something and caught sight of Greg, stopping his words just before they'd formed.

"Hey," Greg said, still friendly as a young malamute. "Look at me. I finally showed up."

Joe looked from his brother to Chynna and back again, not saying a word. Chynna thought she could guess what he was feeling by the look in his eyes, but he didn't say anything. Turning abruptly, he left the room.

"My big brother," Greg explained, nodding toward the doorway. "He's a great guy when he's in a good mood." He grinned. "I just haven't seen him in a good mood for a long, long time. Like, since the day I was born."

Chynna had to laugh, despite everything. Greg and Joe, what a contrast. But they were definitely brothers. She could see the similarities everywhere.

"I guess he's one of those people who needs a cup of coffee before he says anything in the morning," she said, sighing. "Maybe you ought to let me get up so we can go out and all three have a talk."

Greg shrugged. "Sure. Why not? I'll just go stash some of my things in my room. Be back in a second."

She nodded, watching him go. "Oh, my," she whispered to herself. "What now?"

* * *

Joe was tight-lipped, all right. And it wasn't that
there wasn't plenty to say. As he walked stiffly to the
kitchen, he could hardly contain the things welling up
in him. But experience had taught him that saying
them would only make things worse. He had said them
so often before.

What the hell were you thinking? he would have
liked to have said to his brother. *You've got a mother
sitting all alone waiting for you to visit her just once,
and you can't be bothered. She's got a birthday next
week. And I know damn well you're not planning to
do a thing about it. I came to make you go to see her,
but what do I find when I get here? There's a woman
here you promised to marry. But you're not here. You
left her dangling, just like you leave everyone. What
kind of a numskull are you? Can't you keep a commitment to anyone or anything? Can't you honor or
respect any relationship? What's the matter with you?*

He'd been making speeches very like that one to
Greg for years, and it never changed anything. Because deep down, he knew what was the matter with
his brother, knew he'd never change and knew why.
Greg was just like their father.

He filled a glass with water and drank it down
slowly, counting as high as he could, trying to settle
his temper. There was no point in yelling all these
things at Greg. He'd finally learned to hold it back.
But he still hadn't figured out how he could get to his
brother, how he could begin to make him see, begin
to make him change.

He heard Greg's tread in the hallway. He was coming into the kitchen, and Joe steeled himself, but he
still wasn't ready for what his brother had to say next.

"Hey, do you think Annie can perform a wedding

ceremony?'' Greg asked him lightly, slumping into a chair and looking like a happy man. "I mean, she's kind of like unofficial head of the town. If we had a mayor, she'd be it, you know. So why couldn't she marry people? Captains of ships do, don't they?"

"A marriage ceremony?" Joe said, turning to glare at his brother. "What the hell for?"

"For me and Chynna, of course."

For a moment, Joe couldn't speak. Anger choked him. Finally, he croaked out, "You want to marry her?"

"Sure. I wouldn't have sent her the money to come if I didn't want her."

"Then why weren't you here when she arrived?"

Greg grimaced and looked like a kid who'd forgotten to take out the trash. "I would have been, but Jim Barley came by, said there was a brown bear as big as a barn up near Cross Creek Meadow, so I had to go up and take a look. We don't get bear up there anymore, and I had to see what was going on." When he saw the look on Joe's face and realized this explanation wasn't cutting it, his tone became more defensive.

"I was only gone a couple of days. That was hardly anything. You know the trips I usually take. I came back way early..." He thought for a second, trying to find the right word, preferably a word Joe had used to him before on this subject, and then finished his sentence with a pleased smile when he thought of it. "I came back way early to take care of my obligations." He looked up expectantly, obviously hoping for some brotherly praise.

But Joe wasn't ready to reach for compliments just yet. "You've been gone three days," he began.

"Uh-uh. One and a half. I was back last night. I saw you guys at the water hole."

Joe frowned. "Why didn't you make yourself known?"

Greg leaned closer, his face earnest. "Tell you the truth, Joe, when I saw her, I got sort of scared. I mean, she's so beautiful. I was pretty sure her picture in the catalog was rigged. But when I saw she was even prettier than that..." He shook his head. "I gotta admit, for a while there, I lost my nerve."

Joe stared at him, touched by a twinge of compassion for this man of his blood for the first time that day. "What about the kids?" he asked. "Did you see them, too? What do you think?"

Greg shrugged. "They're great. I like kids. This way, I won't have to make my own family. I'll already have one."

Anger swept through Joe again. "What's this all about, Greg? What do you want to do, play house? This is real life you're playing around with."

"I know." His face registered outrage that his motives might be questioned. "I want a wife. I want a family, just like every other guy. I want what every other guy wants."

"Yeah, but you don't want to do what every other guy does to get that."

Greg was beginning to get impatient with Joe's carping. "What else was I supposed to do?" he asked, scratching his head. "I ordered up a wife, and I'm getting kids thrown in free. It seems like a good deal to me."

Joe was slowly shaking his head, his eyes hard as tinted glass. "She won't marry you," he said softly.

Greg looked surprised, then amused. "Sure, she

will. We've got a contract." He gave a short laugh. "Hey, man, you're the lawyer. You know about contracts. They're binding."

Chynna entered the kitchen just in time to hear his last statement. She looked from one brother to the other, her eyes huge and dark. "Well," she said, sinking into a chair at the table, "this changes things."

"No, it doesn't," Joe argued. "It doesn't have to."

She looked up at him, her chin at a challenging angle. "As Greg says, a contract is binding. And we have a contract."

Greg frowned. He could sense something going on underneath their words, something conveyed by the way they were looking at each other, but he wasn't sure what it was.

"Contracts are often broken," Joe said firmly.

"But only for good reason," she countered. "Do you know of a good reason why this one should be?"

He met her gaze and held it. He saw the question in her eyes and he knew what she wanted, but the one thing she wanted was the one thing he couldn't give her. Dragging his attention away, he turned back to Greg.

"Are you coming to see Mother or not?" he asked tersely.

Greg shrugged. "I told you before, I won't go to cities. I'll never set foot in that place. I didn't tell her to move to Anchorage. She should have stayed out here where she belongs."

Joe hesitated. He'd come with plans to hog-tie his brother and drag him back to see his mother if he had to. But circumstances had changed. Everything had changed. Now all he wanted to do was to get out of here.

"Just come for her birthday," he said. "It won't take long. She needs to see you."

Greg smiled, guileless as a child. "How can I go now? I've got a wedding coming up."

That did it. If Joe stayed in the kitchen any longer, he would end up hitting something—very likely his brother's chin. Turning, he grabbed a shirt off a chair and shrugged into it, heading for the front door. Walking out onto the porch, he found himself in the midst of a glorious Alaska morning. The sun was just up, and the birds were coming alive. The air was cool and crystal clear. The snowcapped mountains looked so close, he could almost touch them. Slumping down onto the top step, he sat and drank it all in. He had to admit, this was something magnificent you couldn't get every day in L.A.

He heard someone coming out the front door behind him, but he didn't turn. Still, he was surprised when it was Rusty who sat down beside him, resting his chin in his hands in a direct reflection of Joe's posture.

"Good morning, kid," he said gruffly.

"Good morning," Rusty said back. "Can we go out to look at the animals again?"

Joe smiled at his hopeful face. "Not this morning. Maybe later today." But he knew he wasn't going to be around to take the boy, so why was he setting him up for a letdown? Maybe Greg would take him. For all he knew, Greg was going to be this boy's father soon. He couldn't believe it, but so far no one had told him it wasn't going to happen.

Rusty was looking at his hand, and suddenly he asked, "Remember when I bit you?"

Joe nodded. "I'll never forget it," he promised.

Rusty's gaze shot up to meet his, wary at first, then

smiling when he realized Joe was teasing him. "I wish I didn't do that," he told him earnestly, but before Joe could say anything in return, he'd jumped down from the porch and was running toward the swinging gate.

Suddenly, there was a commotion from around the corner of the house, and before Joe could prepare Rusty, the yard seemed to fill with dogs. In the end, he realized there were only three of them, but they ran so fast and barked so loud and jumped so high, at first it seemed like a lot more. Joe rose, about to go to Rusty and help him, knowing he wasn't used to dogs like this and might be terrified. But Rusty was doing fine. Though he stayed up on the gate, he called to the dogs, and when they came jumping around him, he clung more tightly, but he laughed, and a big black Lab licked his face, delighting him.

These had to be Greg's dogs, and they'd been with him in the mountains, no doubt. Joe had forgotten how friendly dogs could be, how goofy and yet comforting. As he watched them with the boy, he remembered. A boy and a dog. There was sometimes something magic there.

While he was mulling this over, someone else slipped in to sit beside him. Startled, he looked down into Kimmie's tousled hair. She sat very still, just inches away from him, dressed in a pink shirt and tiny jeans, her legs sticking straight out, her feet in little red tennis shoes—and her thumb firmly planted in her mouth. He smiled down at her, and she looked up, but her face was as solemn as ever.

"Won't you smile for me?" he asked her softly.

Slowly and very deliberately, she shook her head.

So he sat beside her, and they both looked out on the morning and watched Rusty with the dogs,

watched him get down off the fence and begin to run
with them. Nothing more was said, but he felt a
strange companionship with the little girl and he had
to admit, it was rather nice having this sort of company—even if she wouldn't smile.

Nine

"Are you really going through with this?" Joe asked as he turned the car down the only main street in town.

"It's starting to look that way, isn't it?" Chynna's eyes danced with excitement. In her hand, she held the key to the building Annie was going to rent to her, if she decided it would suit her needs.

"Well, which is it?" he asked, frowning. "Are you going to start a business or marry Greg?"

She cocked her head to the side as though considering. "I don't know. Can't I do both?" she asked lightly.

After a shocked look in her direction, he lapsed into silence, and she stole a look at his strong profile. Just over two days ago, she hadn't known him. Just over a few hours ago, she hadn't known she loved him. And now...now she was about to lose him. But she wasn't going to let it crush her. She was starting a new life for herself and her babies, and nothing was going to stop her from making that work.

"There it is," he said, pulling the car up in front of a small green building with a front porch and false front. "Do you love it already?"

The funny thing was that she did. It was darling—a little run-down around the edges, but it had a Victorian charm, created mostly by the gingerbread someone had thought important at the time it was built, and the way wildflowers twined around the corners.

"How long has it been empty?" he asked as they got out of the car and walked slowly to the front door.

"A little over a year, Annie said. The couple who had it before ran a sort of trading post, selling Native arts and crafts."

He looked around and shook his head. "This isn't exactly a tourist haven. I don't imagine they got rich."

"No." She laughed. "In fact, they gave up and moved to Florida. Annie says they run a scuba-diving center somewhere on the Keys."

She put the key into the lock, but her hand was shaking and she laughed again as he reached down to help her. The door swung open, and a musty smell came toward them, but the place inside was clean and neat, the front room completely empty, the back rooms completely furnished.

"Oh, look! This will be perfect." She turned, surveying as much as she could from one spot in the middle of the floor. "I wish we'd brought Rusty and Kimmie. They're going to love this."

"Rusty and Kimmie are more interested in baby pigs than they are in real estate," he muttered, frowning as he turned with her. "And Annie's enjoying having them at her place for the moment."

Chynna nodded and began to pace the floor, as though measuring for renovations.

"Look. We can put the counter right here. And the burners back here. And there's already a sink...oh, this is so perfect!"

He watched her and couldn't help but show the trace of a smile. It was pretty clear she had her sights set on starting a business. Where that left his brother he wasn't sure. She'd been very cagey about that ever since Greg had shown up. He couldn't believe she would still consider the marriage, but still, she hadn't definitely ruled it out. Who knew?

"Are you going to have enough money to get this started?" he asked at last, turning to watch her as she examined the room.

She turned and looked at him in surprise. "Don't worry about me. I told you I have some money saved," she said.

He shrugged. "Do you need a loan or anything? Just to get you started."

She did a double take, then stepped closer and searched his face. "Why would you loan me money for this? You hate the whole idea."

He hesitated, then gave her a lopsided grin. "I hate the idea of you failing at it more. So let me know."

She stared at him as he turned away and wandered through the building, looking slightly embarrassed. How could she not love this man? Full of contradictions, yet always basically compassionate, he was also the sexiest man she'd ever seen. Was she crazy to let him slip through her fingers this way?

Sighing, she followed him into the back rooms, which would be the living quarters. The furniture was simple but clean and tasteful. A couch sat against the wall, along with a coffee table and two chairs. There was a dining-room table with six chairs around it, and an empty china cabinet.

"It's going to be perfect," she said again, dreaming of the future. "I'll open the café in the mornings and in the late afternoons. The rest of the time, I'll be preparing food, then I can be with the children, home-schooling them until they're ready for the local school."

He looked up from a book he'd been cradling in his hand. "It's a one-room schoolhouse, you know."

She nodded happily. "Can you imagine? What could be more wonderful?"

He frowned, putting down the book. "I don't know. Most communities seem to think graduated classes with separate teachers for each grade do a better job."

"I don't." She waved an arm in the air. "Just look at what sort of people came out of those little school-houses in the old days. And look at what's coming out of our modern schools these days. I'll take that old-time schoolmarm any day. She knew how to make kids crack the books."

He chuckled. "You may be right," he admitted, enjoying her.

"The thing is," she said, head tilted to the side while she thought it out, "I'll be working out of our home, so I'll always be here when the children are out of school. They will have to help with the work, and good honest work never hurt anyone." She shook her head, her eyes shining. "No, this is going to be everything I've dreamed of."

Her enthusiasm was contagious. He smiled, watching her. "If you feel you've got to do this, I hope you make it."

She turned to him, looking into the depths of his crystal blue eyes. "You do, don't you?" she asked softly.

He nodded. "There's just one thing," he added, his gaze hardening. "Don't marry Greg."

Turning away, she leaned on the windowsill and looked out at the brambles in the backyard. It was going to take a lot of work to clean that up, but she was looking forward to it.

"I'll file your comment away under Biased Advice," she said lightly.

He came up behind her. "You can file it wherever the hell you want to file it, just don't do it."

She licked her lips and pressed them together. "Why shouldn't I marry Greg? It's what I came here to do."

"Because it's wrong for you, it's wrong for the kids and it's darn well wrong for Greg."

She glanced over her shoulder at him. What did he think she was, a fool? Marrying Greg was the last thing on her mind. But she didn't want to tell him. She didn't want it to be too easy.

"Just because marriage isn't your cup of tea..." she began.

Not waiting to hear the rest of it, he seized her shoulders and held her to him.

"Come with me to L.A.," he said impulsively. "You could live with me, you and the kids. You wouldn't have to get an outside job. We could work something out. You could stay home with them and..."

"No," she said firmly, though it cost her a lot to say it. She turned back to look out the window again, and to avoid his eyes. "Don't you understand? That just wouldn't do."

Impatient frustration swept through him. "Why not? Why would marrying Greg be better than that?"

"Because in a marriage, I would be an equal partner. Living with you, the children and I would be supplicants."

He frowned, knowing there was a grain of truth in what she was saying, but refusing to accept it. "That's hogwash."

"No, it's the truth." She shook her head, letting her heavy hair sweep across her back, tiny strands brushing against his face. "I wouldn't live with you without marriage."

He tried to get back to a light note. "Why not? It's all the rage. Everybody's doing it."

She nodded. "And we have a nation filled with lost children who don't know who their parents are. I won't do that to mine."

His hands slid down to curl around her upper arms, caressing them. She felt so good, so clean and healthy and strong. "But you would like to go with me, wouldn't you?" he asked softly. "If there was a way."

She turned her face away, but he forced her to look up at him, holding her chin and turning her.

"You want me, don't you?" he asked her softly, his eyes as deep and darkly blue as a midnight sky. "Tell me the truth."

She touched his face, taking him in with her gaze. "Do I really have to put it into words?" she asked him, her eyes shining. "Can't you feel it?"

He winced, grabbing her hand and putting it over

his heart, holding it there. "You can't marry Greg," he insisted.

She smiled up at him. "Why not?"

He hesitated, but her beautiful face was too close.

"This is why not," he said huskily, drawing her closer.

He told himself he was just going to prove something to her, just wake her up, and then he would release her. He pulled her into his arms, and his mouth closed on hers and all his plans and rationalizations fled. All he knew was her. She melted against him, clung to him, accepting him and giving an answer to his question, and he knew she was right. She didn't have to say it. She knew how to show him with her eyes, her mouth, her body, in ways words could never explain.

It was nice the couch was handy, but it hardly mattered. The hard floor, a sandy beach, rocks in the mountains—it would all have been the same to them. The urgent hunger that filled them both seemed to grow like a wildfire between them, consuming everything in its path. He pulled at her clothes, and she yanked at his, needing to feel her hands against his naked flesh, desperate to feel his lips on her breast, his hand sliding between her legs. It had never been so fierce for her before, and she couldn't stand to be without him. Desire was like a wild thing beating inside her, and only he could tame it.

And he did, rising above her, plunging in and taking control, so that she cried out, her fingers digging into him, her hips churning high in the air to meet him, her eyes wide open as she stared into the fire.

He took her, and it was like nothing he'd ever done before. No woman had made him feel like this. As

they lay together, panting, body parts tangled, he knew
he would never know another woman like her. She
was his, body and soul, and there was no way he could
deny it.

But that didn't make anything different. He was the
same person he'd been before he met her. She was
just as determined to live in Alaska as ever. He looked
down at her, at her beautiful hair spread out across the
pillow, and he wanted to shake her, make her promise
she wouldn't marry his brother, that she wouldn't
marry any man. But he had no right to do that. He
knew very well, if he wasn't willing to offer her anything himself, he couldn't ask her to resist all others.
There was nothing he could do about it.

Still, he could dream.

"You are mine," he whispered fiercely into her
hair.

"What?" She thought he'd said something, but
she'd only heard part of a word. She raised her head
and looked at him. "What did you say?"

"Nothing." He brushed back her hair and looked
at her, and she couldn't tell if the emotion she saw in
his eyes was laughter or something very different.
"Nothing at all."

She nodded slowly. She knew it made no difference.
They could make love all day. They could make love
every time they saw each other. It made no difference.
He was leaving. She was staying behind.

Still, she would always have this. As she traced the
outline of his muscular chest with her fingertip, she
knew that. She would always have a part of him. But
would that ever be enough?

Joe left that evening, driving off in a cloud of dust
that lingered for what seemed like hours. Every time

she looked out the window, she thought she could still see it, particles still floating helplessly in the air with no place to land. But he was gone, and she'd made no promises.

The children didn't ask where he was going, and she didn't know what to tell them, so she ignored the issue and they spent the afternoon playing in the backyard. They were getting to be country kids so quickly, getting used to running free and finding small animals everywhere. It made her heart glad to see them this way.

She'd spent the afternoon cleaning the little building that would be their new home, and now she and the children were spending the evening moving in.

"Why don't you wait until tomorrow?" Greg asked, puzzled at why she would want to leave so quickly. "What's the hurry?"

"I want to be on my own," she told him firmly. "And the children need to have their own rooms."

He frowned, not sure how to take all that. "Now that Joe's gone, we could have really gotten to know each other," he grumped.

She smiled at him. "Come to lunch tomorrow. We'll try out our recipes on you."

That brightened his outlook. "Cool. Could you make me a peanut-butter-and-bacon sandwich? That's my favorite."

"Then that is what you shall have."

She was thrilled to be getting started so quickly. Annie had supplies for the short run, and she would order from distributors Annie recommended in the future. The older woman was also expediting the process of getting a business license and health inspection.

"If only Joe could see me now," she said that night as she surveyed her handiwork—and it was only four hours since he'd left.

But he was constantly in her thoughts. Funny how a man she hardly knew could change her life this way. Funny, but true. Would she ever see him again? She had to believe she would. Somehow—somewhere. She would have to think about it. What she needed was a plan.

Ten

"You're just a big baby, you know." The handsome gray-haired woman looked at her son lovingly across the table in the chic restaurant where they were celebrating her birthday with a trendy nouveau meal. "You have that look on your face you've always had when you didn't get your way."

A rebellious spark flashed in Joe's eyes, but he took a sip of his amber-colored wine and said smoothly, "What could I possibly not be getting my own way about?"

His mother frowned thoughtfully.

"I don't know, but you have that look." She picked up a roll, broke off a piece and buttered it. "Just exactly what happened while you were at Greg's?" she asked with studied indifference.

He grimaced involuntarily. "Nothing. I told you. Greg and I had an argument and he refused to come to Anchorage once again and I left."

She shook her head, pushing back her sleeves and letting her silver bracelets jangle. "I wish you and he would get along better."

He looked up in exasperation. "He's such a flake. What can we do to make him change?"

She smiled. "Nothing. Oh, I know exactly how you feel. Lord knows I've spent enough time trying to make him change myself. But you finally have to face it. Greg is what he is. Accept him that way. Your life will be simpler."

He barely controlled a snarl. "My life is fine. It's his life that's screwed up."

"So let it be. That's Greg." She waited a moment, then went on. "You were there longer than you expected to be."

He nodded, avoiding her eyes. "Yes. When I first arrived, Greg was out hunting. I had to wait for him to reappear."

She smiled, watching him. "And what happened while you were waiting?" she asked quietly.

He met her gaze and hesitated. They'd always been close, and he'd told her a lot about his life. But somehow, he couldn't tell her about this. Not yet.

"Nothing," he lied, looking back down into his drink. "Nothing at all."

But his mother saw the clouds in his gaze and she ached for her son. She had no idea what was troubling him, but she knew it was deep and painful and that it was going to hurt for a long time.

Chynna rested her arm on the ladder for a moment and surveyed the paint job she was doing to her new walls. It looked pretty darn good if she did say so herself. It had been three days since Joe had left, and things were falling into place here at Chynna's Café, as she was thinking of calling it.

Greg was here helping at the moment. He would work for hours if she promised peanut-butter-and-bacon sandwiches at the end of his stint. She watched him work for a moment. He was sanding down shelves they were building to go along the back of the shop. She appreciated the help and enjoyed the company, but he reminded her of Joe, and those reminders were beginning to hurt more. She'd thought they would begin to fade. After all, it wasn't as though he'd become a major part of her life in two days. But he had become a major part of her soul. And in her heart, he seemed to be growing rather than fading away.

As far as she knew, Joe was still in Anchorage visiting with his mother. So near and yet so far.

She glanced down at Greg again as she began to descend the ladder to put away her paintbrush.

"Why won't you go see your mother?" she asked as she went.

He looked up in surprise and then he frowned. "She doesn't really want to see me. She only cares about Joe. He's her favorite."

She didn't know the woman, but she knew women, and she couldn't believe that for a moment. "She cares about you, too. You're her son, her baby."

He shook his shaggy head. "Naw, I was my dad's son. He taught me everything I know about the wilderness."

She began to rinse out her brush. "What about Joe?" she asked above the sound of the water.

Greg shrugged. "What about him?"

"Did he go out into the mountains with you and your dad?"

"Sometimes. But he didn't like hunting. We mostly left him home."

"With your mother." She finished with the rinsing and came over to stand beside where he was working.

"Yeah, they are a lot alike." He made a face and put down the sanding block he'd been using. "Their favorite sport is to sit around and tell me what a loser I am. I don't need to go all the way to a crummy city to have that thrown at me again."

Chynna nodded. So that was it. Well, she could hardly blame him. And yet, everyone pretty much went through that with family. There ought to be some way to get these people together. She frowned, thinking.

"Has she ever visited you since she left? Has she ever come here?"

He shook his head with his lower lip out. "Nope. She left, and that was that." He looked around at where his empty glass was sitting. "You got any more of that chocolate stuff?" he asked.

She went to the thermos and poured out a café mocha for him, thinking all the while. "Maybe you should invite her," she said as she handed him the drink.

Greg nearly dropped it. "Who? Me?"

She gazed at him speculatively. "How about if I do it?" She began to get excited by her own idea. "Why don't we have a birthday party for her right here? We could invite Annie and all her old friends."

He stared at her, then shrugged. "Well, if you think so. I guess it would be okay."

She smiled, charged up now. They already had phone service hooked up to the café. It was about time she used it. "This will be great. Give me her phone number. I'll call her right away."

She glanced at Greg as he obligingly began to look through his wallet for the number. Would he think this through? Would he consider the fact that Joe was probably still there? Would she blow her cover?

It wasn't as if she'd plotted here. The idea had just fallen into her lap. But she would run with it now. And maybe, just maybe, something would come of it. Unless Greg realized...

But no. He found the number and handed it to her. "Tell her hi for me," he said casually as she walked toward the other room, where the telephone was kept. "She's pretty nice, actually."

Chynna's heart was beating like a drum as she listened to the telephone ring. What if Joe answered?

But it was a woman's voice she heard on the other end of the line.

"Mrs. Camden? You don't know me, but I know your sons."

"Oh?"

"Yes. You see..." Suddenly, she realized that this was going to be very awkward to explain. "I came to Alaska to marry Greg, but..."

"What? Where did you meet my son?"

"I didn't. I mean..." She sighed. The truth was the only way. "I came as a mail-order bride. But Greg wasn't here and Joe arrived and waited with me for Greg to come back, and by the time Greg came back...well..."

"You are no longer planning to marry Greg." The woman made it a statement of fact, and Chynna couldn't dispute it. She glanced toward the front room, but Greg was out of hearing distance.

"No. I'm not going to marry him. But I've gotten to know both your sons very well, Mrs. Camden, and I know how much they care for you. The thing is...I would like to have a birthday party for you here in Dunmovin.''

There was a moment of silence while she absorbed this. ''Why would you do that?''

''Because I think you should see Greg.''

She paused, then asked, ''Why can't he come see me here?''

Her fingers tightened on the receiver. ''I think he would like to, Mrs. Camden. But I think he's just too close to the wild to make the trip. It breaks my heart to see a rift between a mother and child. I have two children of my own. So I'd like to try to do something for the two of you. Will you come?''

Mrs. Camden was silent for a long moment. Finally, she spoke. ''Yes, my dear,'' she said firmly. ''I will come.''

Chynna's heart leaped. They went over the particulars of the time and place, and when she hung up, she was glowing. Joe's mother was coming. She hadn't had the nerve to ask if Joe would be coming with her. But at one point, she'd heard his voice in the background. Surely he would come. Surely.

Joe looked out the small airplane window at the city below. L.A. He was coming home. Alaska was like a dream to him now. He'd been thinking over what his mother had told him about Greg, that he had to accept his brother the way he was, and he was beginning to come to terms with it. Finding out that Chynna wasn't going to marry him had helped enormously. Somehow, he could feel much friendlier toward him now. Would he ever be able to be around him and not be annoyed? Probably not. But he thought he was getting over the need to try to reform him. He had to admit, chances were it was no use.

But now he was back in California and he could forget all that. He only wished he were looking forward to getting back to work more. He'd enjoyed legal work for a long time, but lately things had gone very stale. He needed something new to pep him up. Something to start his blood flowing again.

"Please fasten your seat belt, Mr. Camden," the pretty redheaded flight attendant asked. "We'll be landing in a few minutes."

She'd been flirting with him all the way from Seattle. As he leaned back in his seat he watched her tight little bottom wiggle down the aisle. *Ask her out,* a voice said. *Come on. She's given you every signal. Ask her out and go have some fun.*

Okay. He was ready. The next time she came this way, he would do it. *Would you join me for dinner?* he would say, very suave and confident. She was coming back down the aisle. He got his smile ready. He was going to do it.

The plane hit a pocket and gave a jolt, and she turned back, bracing herself with the back of a seat some distance away. And at the same time, a little girl jumped up, out of her seat, and tried to run down the aisle herself. Her mother called her back sharply, leaning out to do so, and Joe got a good look at them both. They could have been Chynna and Kimmie, both so blond, both so sweet looking. The flight attendant came his way again, throwing him a dazzling smile. But he barely noticed and barely returned it. His mind was back in Alaska. Back in the dream.

There would be no dinner with the flight attendant. He only hoped he'd be able to eat at all.

Chynna and Greg were making preparations for the party, blowing up balloons and tacking down stream-

ers. The whole town had gotten involved. Everyone
was coming. Chynna was having a hard time holding
back her excitement. Her new life was starting off with
a bang. The party and her grand opening were coin-
ciding. The icing on the cake would be if Joe came.
But that was almost too much to hope for, wasn't it?
In the meantime, she babbled on and on about her
plans to Greg, until he grew a bit testy.

"Now, wait a minute," he demanded at one point.
"What about us?"

"What *about* us?" she returned, blinking at him.

He frowned at her. "Are we getting married or
what?"

She drew in a deep breath. She'd been expecting
this conversation for days, and now it was finally here.
She had to be honest with him. "Greg, I'm very sorry,
but I don't think we should do that."

His blue eyes widened. "But you promised."

She took his hand in hers. "I know I promised. And
I'm very sorry. But you know, if you look at the contract, you'll see that there is a back-door clause in case
either one of us gets cold feet."

"You've got cold feet?"

She nodded. "Freezing," she murmured.

He looked more confused than angry. "So, there's
a clause in there for me, too?" he asked her.

She looked at him for a moment, then laughed.
"You didn't really want to marry me, either, did
you?" she accused.

But he denied it. Well, he halfway denied it. "Sure,
I did. Only..." He flushed and avoided her gaze.
"Only I saw Nancy last night, and she heard all about
you and she was real impressed." He looked very
pleased with himself. "The way she was making eyes

at me, I figure I might have a chance with her after all.''

She stared at him with her mouth open. ''Why, you little devil. If I find out you dragged me all the way to Alaska just to make Nancy jealous—''

''Oh, no. Oh, I swear that wasn't why.''

''—I'll be grateful to you until the day I die. Coming up here was the best thing I ever did.''

He blinked. ''Oh.'' He blinked again. ''Okay, then I guess it *was* my fault.''

With a shriek, she attacked him and they wrestled for a moment, both laughing, both feeling more like brother and sister than anything else. But it brought back memories of wrestling with Joe. And the contrast was startling. So much so that later that night, she watched the faint stars and wished on one.

''Please make Joe come back,'' she whispered.

Did wishes get granted in Alaska? She would soon find out.

It seemed that in Alaska, wishing on stars didn't work. Maybe it was because of the short nights. At any rate, Mrs. Camden arrived for her party without her oldest son in tow, and Chynna's heart sank when she realized it.

Still, it was touching to see Mrs. Camden's reunion with Greg, who actually shaved for the occasion. It was especially heartwarming when his eyes filled with tears as his mother hugged him. His crusty defenses shattered in that moment, and as the evening wore on, he was the life of the party, and especially dazzling when the lovely Nancy was nearby.

Mrs. Camden herself had a wonderful time. People came from miles around to see her, and she was astounded at how much she'd been missed.

"I'll be back again soon," she promised everyone. "I won't stay away so long next time."

There was dancing and singing and lots and lots of food. Chynna was already feeling like an old-time member of the community. Annie had taken her under her wing, and that was enough for most residents. One after another, mountain men came by to tell her they would be trying her sandwiches on their next trips. And everyone was looking forward to her cappuccino concoctions.

As the evening wended its way toward midnight, she had a chance for a talk with Joe's mother. They felt a bond immediately, and Mrs. Camden didn't waste any time.

"Are you in love with my son?" she asked.

Chynna stammered. "I...I thought I explained...."

"I don't mean Greg," she said. "What have you done to Joe?"

"Done to him?" She realized she was blushing. It was too late to deny anything.

"Yes, done to him. He was mooning around like a love-sick puppy. Well, out with it. What happened?"

Chynna gave her a brief outline, leaving out a lot of details, but including the fact that she'd never known a man like him.

"He's so strong, and yet so good and kind," she told his mother, as if she didn't know the fellow herself. "I don't understand why he won't consider staying here where he grew up. I would think he would love it."

Mrs. Camden nodded. "Joe felt, all his life, that Greg was like his father, made for Alaska, and that he was like me. He felt out of place here. When he was young, he was sure there were things out there in the rest of the world that would suit him better. He could hardly wait to leave." She sighed, thinking of the old days. "But he's been gone a long time now. I think his sense of alienation went too far, and it's time for him to realize that. Alaska is in his blood, just as much as it's in Greg's."

Chynna hesitated. "Well, if that's true, he won't admit it."

Mrs. Camden smiled. "We might have to trick him into it," she said softly. "Do you have a telephone? I'm feeling a little light-headed. I think I'd better make a call to my son in California."

Chynna watched, holding her breath, as the woman left the room and headed for the telephone. She wasn't sure this was going to work. But what the heck. It was worth a try. Anything to get the man back in town.

Joe hit the road to Dunmovin at eighty miles per hour, swearing all the way. He didn't want to do this. He'd just left Alaska. He hadn't wanted to come back.

But as he drove along the highway, he couldn't help but see the landscape, and he couldn't keep from being enchanted by it again. Was there any place on earth as beautiful?

Alaska was a big country. A man ought to be able to do big things here.

He pulled into town, driving right past Annie's. His mother had said she was staying with Chynna at the café, and that made him swear again. How the hell had those two got together and got so cozy so fast?

Pulling up in the driveway, he got out of the car and stretched, stiff from the long drive. He heard the sound of running feet and turned to find Rusty coming out on the porch.

"Wow," the boy called out, eyes wide. "It's Joe. You came back."

Joe moved awkwardly, wishing kids weren't so darn vulnerable. "Just for a visit," he said quickly, but Rusty didn't seem to hear him.

"Did you come back to be our daddy?" he asked, as though it were the most natural question in the world.

Words stuck in Joe's throat. He couldn't have been more shocked if Rusty had shot him. He had to reach out and put a hand on the gate to steady himself, and then he heard his own voice saying, "Do you want me to be your daddy?"

The world seemed to stand still. The air didn't move; the sun held its breath. And Rusty's eyes clouded for a moment, as though he wasn't sure he should answer that. He thought for a moment, staring at Joe, mulling over the question.

Finally, he bobbed his head shyly. "Kimmie does," he said brightly. "She told me."

Joe turned, feeling like a man in a dream, moving in slow motion, because Kimmie was coming through the doorway, and when she saw him, her thumb popped out of her mouth and she cried out, "Joe!" and dashed toward him.

He wasn't sure how it happened, if she leaped into the air or if he reached down and swung her up, but she was in his bear hug of an embrace and her little arms were around his neck and she was saying, "Joe, Joe," over and over, and when he drew back and looked at her, she was smiling.

His eyes were stinging, and at first he didn't know why. But he couldn't let that little girl go, not until her mother was there, walking toward him, and then his sense of the surreal went into overdrive.

It was like one of those movies, he thought later, where the man and the woman come together across a field full of daisies, where they see one another in the distance and just start moving together, like two halves of a whole that must unite. All he had to see was the deep darkness of her eyes and he was drowning in them, reaching for her, taking her up in his arms.

She was crying. Her face was wet and—funny thing, so was his. But he was kissing away the tears, kissing her again and again, kissing her eyes and her nose and her lips and her ears, until his lips were sore from the kissing and she was laughing and pulling away. The kids were hanging on to his legs, one on each, and they were laughing and he was laughing and it all happened without warning. He found his family and bonded with them, and no one had told him it would be like this. But by the time he'd realized what had happened, it was too late to stop. He heard his own voice telling Chynna he loved her, so where could he go from there?

"Why not have the wedding right here in Clarks' meadow?" his mother was saying, referring to the yard behind the café. He didn't care where it was because the wedding was a thing for women to plan, and all he cared about was that he would have Chynna with him for the rest of his life and that her kids would be his.

"You can live in Alaska?" Chynna was asking him, and he could tell he was nodding yes, though he wasn't sure why.

"Computers make everything easier," he heard his voice saying. "I can work here. I love Alaska."

"Good," his mother said, and he vaguely remembered that she was supposed to be having fainting spells or something, wasn't that what had brought him here? But she looked okay now, walking off across the meadow with the kids to give the two of them some time alone. And as Chynna drew him to her and wrapped him in her arms, he sighed and shook his head.

"I'm not really sure how all this happened," he told her, looking a little bewildered.

She laughed deep in her throat. "Just consider yourself a mail-order husband," she teased him. "I ordered you up, and here you are."

He dropped a kiss on her lips, and somehow it grew and wouldn't quit. This was what he'd been missing all his life. Funny how long it had taken him to admit it.

"I love you," he told her huskily, her face between his hands.

"I love you, too," she told him, her eyes filling with happy tears. "We all do."

"Even Kimmie?"

"Especially Kimmie." She gave him a ragged smile and pulled him closer. "No, I take that back," she whispered as her body melted into his. "Especially me."

And he wouldn't have had it any other way.

*   *   *   *   *

SILHOUETTE WOMEN KNOW ROMANCE WHEN THEY SEE IT.

And they'll see it on **ROMANCE CLASSICS**, the new 24-hour TV channel devoted to romantic movies and original programs like the special **Romantically Speaking—Harlequin™ Goes Prime Time.**

Romantically Speaking—Harlequin™ Goes Prime Time introduces you to many of your favorite romance authors in a program developed exclusively for Harlequin® and Silhouette® readers.

Watch for **Romantically Speaking—Harlequin™ Goes Prime Time** beginning in the summer of 1997.

If you're not receiving ROMANCE CLASSICS, call your local cable operator or satellite provider and ask for it today!

Escape to the network of your dreams.

ROMANCE CLASSICS

See Ingrid Bergman and Gregory Peck in *Spellbound* on Romance Classics.

Take 4 bestselling love stories FREE

Plus get a FREE surprise gift!

Special Limited-time Offer

Mail to Silhouette Reader Service™

3010 Walden Avenue
P.O. Box 1867
Buffalo, N.Y. 14240-1867

YES! Please send me 4 free Silhouette Desire® novels and my free surprise gift. Then send me 6 brand-new novels every month, which I will receive months before they appear in bookstores. Bill me at the low price of $2.90 each plus 25¢ delivery and applicable sales tax, if any.* That's the complete price and a savings of over 10% off the cover prices—quite a bargain! I understand that accepting the books and gift places me under no obligation ever to buy any books. I can always return a shipment and cancel at any time. Even if I never buy another book from Silhouette, the 4 free books and the surprise gift are mine to keep forever.

225 BPA A3UU

Name	(PLEASE PRINT)	
Address	Apt. No.	
City	State	Zip

This offer is limited to one order per household and not valid to present Silhouette Desire® subscribers. *Terms and prices are subject to change without notice.
Sales tax applicable in N.Y.

UDES-696

©1990 Harlequin Enterprises Limited

**Help us celebrate
15 years of unforgettable
romance with**

SILHOUETTE®

Desire®

You could win a genuine lead crystal vase, or one of 4 sets of 4 crystal champagne flutes! Every prize is made of hand-blown, hand-cut crystal, with each process handled by master craftsmen. We're making these fantastic gifts available to be won by you, just for helping us celebrate 15 years of the best romance reading around!

DESIRE CRYSTAL SWEEPSTAKES
OFFICIAL ENTRY FORM

To enter, complete an Official Entry Form or 3" x 5" card by hand printing the words "Desire Crystal Sweepstakes," your name and address thereon and mailing it to: in the U.S., Desire Crystal Sweepstakes, P.O. Box 9076, Buffalo, NY 14269-9076; in Canada, Desire Crystal Sweepstakes, P.O. Box 637, Fort Erie, Ontario L2A 5X3. Limit: one entry per envelope, one prize to an individual, family or organization. Entries must be sent via first-class mail and be received no later than 12/31/97. No responsibility is assumed for lost, late, misdirected or nondelivered mail.

DESIRE CRYSTAL SWEEPSTAKES
OFFICIAL ENTRY FORM

Name: _____

Address: _____

City: _____

State/Prov.: _____ Zip/Postal Code: _____

KFO

15YRENTRY

Desire Crystal Sweepstakes
Official Rules—No Purchase Necessary

To enter, complete an Official Entry Form or 3" x 5" card by hand printing the words "Desire Crystal Sweepstakes," your name and address thereon and mailing it to: in the U.S., Desire Crystal Sweepstakes, P.O. Box 9076, Buffalo, NY 14269-9076; in Canada, Desire Crystal Sweepstakes, P.O. Box 637, Fort Erie, Ontario L2A 5X3. Limit: one entry per envelope, one prize to an individual, family or organization. Entries must be sent via first-class mail and be received no later than 12/31/97. No responsibility is assumed for lost, late, misdirected or nondelivered mail.

Winners will be selected in random drawings (to be conducted no later than 1/31/98) from among all eligible entries received by D. L. Blair, Inc., an independent judging organization whose decisions are final. The prizes and their approximate values are: Grand Prize—a Mikasa Crystal Vase ($140 U.S.); 4 Second Prizes—a set of 4 Mikasa Crystal Champagne Flutes ($50 U.S. each set).

Sweepstakes offer is open only to residents of the U.S. (except Puerto Rico) and Canada who are 18 years of age or older, except employees and immediate family members of Harlequin Enterprises, Ltd., their affiliates, subsidiaries and all other agencies, entities and persons connected with the use, marketing or conduct of this sweepstakes. All applicable laws and regulations apply. Offer void wherever prohibited by law. Taxes and/or duties on prizes are the sole responsibility of the winners. Any litigation within the province of Quebec respecting the conduct and awarding of a prize in this sweepstakes may be submitted to the Régie des alcools, des courses et des jeux. All prizes will be awarded; winners will be notified by mail. No substitution for prizes is permitted. Odds of winning are dependent upon the number of eligible entries received.

Any prize or prize notification returned as undeliverable may result in the awarding of that prize to an alternative winner. By acceptance of their prize, winners consent to use of their names, photographs or likenesses for purposes of advertising, trade and promotion on behalf of Harlequin Enterprises, Ltd., without further compensation unless prohibited by law. In order to win a prize, residents of Canada will be required to correctly answer a time-limited, arithmetical skill-testing question administered by mail.

For a list of winners (available after January 31, 1998), send a separate stamped, self-addressed envelope to: Desire Crystal Sweepstakes 5309 Winners, P.O. Box 4200, Blair, NE 68009-4200, U.S.A.

Sweepstakes sponsored by Harlequin Enterprises Ltd., P.O. Box 9042, Buffalo, NY 14269-9042.

15YRRULE

As seen on TV!
Free Gift Offer

With a Free Gift proof-of-purchase from any Silhouette® book,
you can receive a beautiful cubic zirconia pendant.

This gorgeous marquise-shaped stone is a genuine cubic
zirconia—accented by an 18" gold tone necklace.

(Approximate retail value $19.95)

Send for yours today...
compliments of ♥ *Silhouette*®
™

To receive your free gift, a cubic zirconia pendant, send us one original proof-of-
purchase, photocopies not accepted, from the back of any Silhouette Romance™,
Silhouette Desire®, Silhouette Special Edition®, Silhouette Intimate Moments®
or Silhouette Yours Truly™ title available at your favorite retail outlet, together with
the Free Gift Certificate, plus a check or money order for $1.65 U.S./$2.15 CAN. (do
not send cash) to cover postage and handling, payable to Silhouette Free Gift Offer.
We will send you the specified gift. Allow 6 to 8 weeks for delivery. Offer good until
December 31, 1997, or while quantities last. Offer valid in the U.S. and Canada only.

Free Gift Certificate

Name: _____

Address: _____

City: _____ State/Province: _____ Zip/Postal Code: _____

Mail this certificate, one proof-of-purchase and a check or money order for postage
and handling to: SILHOUETTE FREE GIFT OFFER 1997. In the U.S.: 3010 Walden
Avenue, P.O. Box 9077, Buffalo NY 14269-9077. In Canada: P.O. Box 613, Fort Erie,
Ontario L2Z 5X3.

FREE GIFT OFFER   084-KFD
ONE PROOF-OF-PURCHASE
To collect your fabulous FREE GIFT, a cubic zirconia pendant, you must include this
original proof-of-purchase for each gift with the properly completed Free Gift Certificate.

084-KFDR

SILHOUETTE DESIRE
FIFTEEN YEARS OF FANTASY MEN!

Who can resist a Desire hero? No one! They're the men that fantasies are made of—handsome, rugged, caring and sexy. In November 1997 watch for:

ANN MAJOR as she continues her bestselling Children of Destiny series with *Nobody's Child.* This Man of the Month is a business tycoon who will melt your heart!

Ranchin' Men! In *Journey's End* by **BJ JAMES**, a rancher heals our soul-weary heroine with the power of love. This is part of BJ's bestselling series, The Black Watch. Talented author **EILEEN WILKS** is going to show us how *Cowboys Do It Best* in this sultry tale of seduction.

**Marriage!
LASS SMALL's
*How To Win (Back) a Wife***
reunites an estranged married couple who fell out of love from a hasty wedding. A sexy attorney hears wedding bells in *Marriage on His Mind* by **SUSAN CROSBY**. And in *Wyoming Wife?* by **SHAWNA DELACORTE,** our hero has to convince a damsel in distress to be his bride.

Silhouette Desire...what better way to meet so many gorgeous guys?

Available November 1997, at your favorite retail outlet.